HOW WE SELL OUR SOULS

In the Darkness, Book One

Emilie Lucadamo

A NineStar Press Publication

Published by NineStar Press
P.O. Box 91792,
Albuquerque, New Mexico, 87199 USA.
www.ninestarpress.com

How We Sell Our Souls

Printed in the USA
First Edition
November, 2018

Print ISBN: 978-1-949909-47-0

Also available in eBook, ISBN: 978-1-949909-44-9

Warning: This book contains sexual content, which may only be suitable for mature readers, death of minor characters and some gore.

When George Soto turns twenty-six, his life is less than perfect. Stuck in a dead-end job, watching his friends pass him by, it's quickly starting to feel like he's going nowhere. When he finds a strange ritual meant to contract a demon, he doesn't imagine it could possibly work.

Until there's a demon standing in his living room.

George doesn't know what a contract with a demon entails, but it seems like a great opportunity to get revenge on his awful boss. Gradually, he and the demon—an abrasive entity who calls himself Jack—form an alliance.

But as things heat up between them, George almost doesn't notice the increasing darkness in his life. The nights are longer, the shadows grow heavier, and the world around him seems to be distorting.

To Amruta—who gave me a small idea, which sprawled into a frightening, wild thing. From here on out, let's be proud of each other.

Chapter One

BITTER ALCOHOL RUNS down his throat, burning like liquid fire. It's sheer force of will that keeps George from choking, even though he's sure what he's drinking has got to be at least half ethanol, half nail polish remover. He slams the shot glass on the table and sputters, struggling to breathe past the burning in his throat. Tears pool at the corners of his eyes; he blinks them away to the sound of his friends' raucous laughter.

"One more down the hatch!" Matt exclaims. "Keep this up and you might catch up with us!"

"Might," echoes Alex. "Optimism is a beautiful thing."

George wipes the tears from his eyes before narrowing them at his friends. He can take a joke as well as the next guy, but after the day he's had he'd prefer a little sympathy.

"Come on, jerks, quit harping on me just because I got here late."

"An hour late," interjects Josh, like this is a point of extreme incredulity. "To your own birthday party."

George snorts, glancing around at the motley assembly of the three friends who make up his "party"—Matt with his hair mussed, Alex hanging half off his barstool, and Josh slamming another empty shot glass on the table. "You guys are the best I could get for my birthday? Oh man, my life *is* tragic."

Josh reaches over and punches him in the arm. It shouldn't hurt, except Josh sometimes doesn't realize his own strength, so it hurts a lot. George subtly shifts his numbing arm as he swipes at the other man. Across from him, Matt is laughing again. Maybe it's the alcohol settling into his veins, or maybe Matt's laugh is just so damn contagious, but George finds himself grinning back.

He can feel his foul mood fading away, and he's glad for it. It's not like getting a mountain of paperwork forced on you by your boss is a weak reason to be pissed off. Still, it's his damn birthday—he deserves to have a good time.

"Sawyer's an ass," Matt says, still snickering as he reaches for a shot of his own. "It's not like this is a surprise."

"Still. He had to have known you'd have plans," Josh pipes up. It's true; they have an office birthday calendar, and people have been congratulating George on having made it through another year all day long. (Not Sawyer, of course, but George's jaw would have hit the floor if his boss had.)

"Like I said: ass," Matt says, at the same time Alex mutters, "Satan incarnate."

Matt slams the shot glass on the table, remaining still for a few seconds as the burn of alcohol fades away. His sharp hiccup dissolves into a round of snickering. The flush on Matt's face reminds George that his friends have been drinking for a solid hour longer than he has. He finds himself moving to snatch his own shot from the tray before anyone else can get to it. The last thing he wants is to end up the most sober person at his own party.

He tosses back the alcohol and winds up coughing, stunned by the burn of fiery liquid. He's got no clue what these shots are, but for the way they taste he hopes they cost his friends a small fortune.

"Take it easy," Alex mutters to Matt, who's still giggling. "If you pass out, no one's dragging your sorry ass back home."

"We'll just call Lila to come get you," Josh says with a wicked grin. The threat has the desired sobering effect. Matt blanches and shrinks back into his seat.

"God, no. Last time she chewed me out, I couldn't stand to look at myself for days. That woman has a way of tearing you down and putting you back together again with nothing but her disapproval and the brute force of your own shame."

He shudders. George and Josh exchange sly looks, and both lean forward in anticipation. It's only a few seconds before Matt's disturbed expression melts into something gentle, and he smirks down at the table. "God, I love her."

Alex rolls his eyes. George reaches for another shot with one hand, high fiving Josh with the other. "Every time!"

There are several guarantees every time he goes out drinking with his buddies. At some point, he and Josh will get into a drinking competition (*"I'm Irish, Soto, you don't stand a chance,"* Josh always says, before being soundly outdrunk by George). Whatever food they order will be thrown around. Two people will get into an argument about something stupid. And Matt will wax poetic about the love of his life, Lila Cooper.

George presses an empty glass to his lips and grins into it. He might be a year older, but some things never change. Even if they're all getting older now, and it seems like very few things want to stay the way they have always been.

It makes sense, of course. They're not college students anymore. Alex isn't top of his class; instead, he's slaving away behind a desk at a publishing agency. Josh has stopped dreaming of being a journalist and is actually trying to get there. Matt's doing his damnedest to carve out a life for himself, whether it be clawing his way up at his firm or proposing to his longtime girlfriend. It seems as if everybody's life is on a rapid collision course with new and better things—the only one staying right where he's always been is George.

The worst part is, he's not sure he wants it any other way. Maybe things are better if they don't change at all. Change is risky—you don't know what it could bring. After all, he's happy enough where he is now, right?

Sure he is. His life is great. He doesn't have anything to complain about, except for his miserable boss. Everything else is fine. It's goddamn great.

Happy birthday to me, he thinks, before raising his arm to order another round of shots.

Screw Sawyer and his paperwork. Screw his crummy job. Screw being twenty-six and single, his closest friends being his old college buddies, and his useless cat.

Tonight is his party, and he's going to have a good time if it kills him.

IT IS WELL past midnight by the time the group finally stumbles out of the bar. They must look ridiculous, swaying on their feet, snorting with laughter and muttering to each other as they giggle into the night air. George supports himself against Josh or Alex, swaying between the two and clinging to their arms whenever he needs the help staying upright. On Alex's other side, Matt is listing heavily against the buildings as they pass them, staining his shirt sleeve with brick dust as he drags his body along.

"It's cold," George mutters, even though it's June, and it really isn't. "Am I the only one who's really freaking cold?"

"Yes," Alex says, and then makes a noise of disgruntlement as George grips onto his shoulder for balance. Matt snickers again, and nearly winds up toppling over. They all stop in the middle of the sidewalk for a second to watch him regain his balance, arms flailing and feet scrabbling for purchase. When he finally does, he lifts his head with a glowing sort of victory. George thinks it would be better suited for a conquering hero than a drunk guy who managed to not fall on his ass, but Matt has a penchant for the dramatic.

Once they've ascertained they aren't about to lose Matt to the comforts of a hard sidewalk, they stumble on. George has no clue where they're going; his place, maybe, since his apartment is the closest, but he's pretty sure they're still blocks away. No one thought to get a taxi when they left the bar, apparently, because walking long distances while drunk is *so much fun.*

George trips over an invisible crack in the sidewalk and curses as he almost goes sprawling. Jesus Christ, he should have called a damn Uber.

"Ah man, I have to pee," says Josh. He lets a few seconds pass in silence before repeating himself, only to reassure them that nothing's changed, "I have to pee so bad."

"Shut up, Josh. Just. Shut up," Matt mutters, bracing himself against the brick building as he sways. "Now I'm gonna have to go too."

"I need to *pee.*"

"Peeing's for the weak," Matt says.

"Next person who says pee, I'll kick 'em," declares Alex, swinging his fist in a clumsy arc for good measure. Alex is a grouchy drunk. He's not surly, and he won't actually fight anyone (most of the time), but he's got no problem telling people to shut up. He also has zero depth perception, so any actual attempts to fight someone would end poorly. George keeps an eye on Drunk Alex, because he's a riot without meaning to be.

"Just go in the street," George mutters. At this point, he's tired of hearing them talk about it.

This seems to be good enough for Josh, who turns to the closest alleyway and lets his hands drift to his pants. Well damn, George wasn't actually serious. He opens his mouth to intervene, but Matt gets there first, pushing himself off from the wall to throw an arm around Josh's shoulders. "No, no no," he says. "This is how we get arrested."

Josh frowns at him, then down at his half-zipped fly. "But I have to go."

He's not going to shut up until he's able to go, and everyone knows this. George begins scanning the mostly-dark street in the vain hope of finding somewhere that hasn't yet closed for the night. A post office, a restaurant—hell, even a gift shop would be good enough, as long as it has a bathroom.

Most of the shops on the street are locked up tight, windows darkened and sign on the doors flipped to Closed. Big surprise, and just George's luck, too—now he's going to have to listen to Josh whine for another however-many blocks.

That's when his gaze lands on what has to be an actual God-given miracle—or, at least as close as you can get to that in urban Rhode Island. It's a little bookshop devoid of any sign on the door, or any indication it hasn't closed up yet. The store window is piled with mountains of books, but behind them, the light is clearly on. It is a beacon on the otherwise dark street, warm glow singing out to George's drunken mind.

"Hey," he says, pointing towards the shop. "Try there, it's still open."

Josh looks that way, and his face lights up. He's not the only one who's relieved. Alex mutters a "Thank God," as he follows Josh down the sidewalk, and Matt runs a hand through his hair as he trails behind them at a more sedate pace. George huffs what isn't quite a laugh, following his friends to the friendly looking little shop at the end of the street.

They push open the door to the light sound of bells. George's gaze drifts up to the instrument fixed on top of the door; it is a glowing silver bell, engraved with black symbols he's too short and too drunk to make out. It's a nice bell, he thinks. Nicer than anything where he works, including the computers. (God, his office has shitty computers. Maybe this place is hiring?)

He's just starting to drift down a weird road of thought when a door behind the counter opens, and a figure steps out. It's a slender young man, clothed in shadow. He wears a gray button-down and black jeans, matching the shade of his hair exactly. His eyes shine like two hot coals, and black stains the palms of his hands; it takes George a bit too long to realize this is ink. The only thing remotely colorful about the guy is his skin, a warm brown that stands out against his monochrome clothing. Dark circles rest under eyes that regard the group in the middle of his shop with wariness.

That gaze reminds him of being scrutinized at work. Unconsciously, George straightens up and offers the bookstore owner his best smile.

"Hi," he says. The owner frowns.

"Sorry, we're closed for tonight."

The thing that hits George first is the preciseness of his words. The guy sounds like he's trying to cover up an accent but isn't quite managing it. Every syllable is pronounced. Still, this does nothing to distract from the silken smoothness of his tone, like liquid metal running down a slanted surface. It washes over George, stirring faint, unfamiliar memories of someplace far away from here.

"We figured." Matt's making his best effort to be charming too, giving the owner his best smile. "We just wondered if we could use your bathroom?"

The guy takes in the swaying cluster of drunk men in his shop for a few more seconds before he shakes his head, slow and cautious. "Sorry, boys. I can't let you in here right now. I'm a little busy."

He gestures with his hands to the mountains of books and papers littering the counter. It's a complete mess, though it honestly doesn't seem out of place with the rest of the store. George glances at the array, and his eyebrows shoot up. The guy isn't joking about being busy. This is more work than Sawyer threw at him tonight.

There are stray pages scattered everywhere, with drawings and symbols liberally spread throughout them. He can't help noticing the pen on the table and a few papers that look half written. Is the guy writing a book or something? George frowns, taking a step closer without realizing, but he's blocked by Alex's body suddenly in his way.

"Sorry, we know it's late—" Alex starts, ever the diplomat. "Like, really late—and you didn't ask for a buncha drunk idiots in your shop—"

"Hey, what're you?" demands George.

"But we'd really appreciate it."

"He'll pee his pants," George sees fit to contribute. "He's done it before." The glare Josh sends him could burn a hole in the floor, but George has been on the receiving end of drunk slander from him enough times that he isn't a bit sorry.

The bookstore owner glances between the group, taking in the obvious desperation on Josh's face and the tipsy friendliness on Matt and Alex's. Maybe he decides they're pitiful, or at least too drunk to be much more than a nuisance, but he finally buckles with a beleaguered sigh. "All right," he says, gesturing to the back of the store. "Come on, whoever's gotta go can go."

Josh breaks out into a wide grin. George huffs in relief, glad he won't have to listen to his friend's complaining all night; his attention is still focused on the papers littering the counter. The bookstore owner doesn't notice as he begins to lead the group back, opening the door behind the counter to a dimly lit hallway. "Okay, buddy system," Matt declares, clumsily clapping Josh on the back. "Let's go, buddy."

"Pal," Josh says before almost tripping over his own feet.

Alex snorts, taking the rear in case either one of them decides to topple over. The poor bookshop owner doesn't deserve to deal with *that,* on top of the drunk nuisances crashing his place in the middle of the night.

"Come on, man," Alex says, but George waves a hand at him.

"I'm gonna wait outside. Don't take too long."

He holds his breath until the door shuts behind them with a click. He waits a second, listening to the thud of footsteps moving down the hallway. There is no danger of anyone coming back. He's alone.

George has no clue why he was waiting for that, but as soon as he's certain he's got the room to himself, he springs into action. He was brought up right; his mother always told him not to snoop, and to never touch things that don't belong to him.

Unfortunately, George has always been an insufferably curious bastard. He's never been good at keeping his nose out of other people's business.

He hears a door in the back of the shop click shut, and that settles it. He's moving before he knows it, peering over the desk to take in the mass of papers there.

He couldn't say why he was intrigued by them from a distance. Maybe he was curious as to exactly what this poor guy was working on to keep him at work until one in the morning. Maybe his drunk brain just thought the drawings looked cool. He really couldn't say; but as he gets closer, it becomes obvious he's looking at something he couldn't have anticipated.

A lot of the half-scribbled pages seem to be written in code—a strange alphabet of jaunty symbols he can't make heads or tails of. He peers at them for a moment, frowning, before moving on to the nearest page in English.

This is a strange one: *Methods Of Gathering Graveyard Dirt.*

"The hell?" George mutters to himself before moving on. There's a well-worn page titled *Circle Casting Rituals.* Another goes into detail about various herbs used to cure stomach aches. There are entire books talking about moon phases, guides to plants and spices, and pages devoted to various healing rituals. It's like he's stumbled upon the weird collection of a cross between an herbalist and a witch doctor.

He pulls off his glasses and presses his fingers over his eyes, as if hoping the spells will be gone when he opens them up again. He's out of luck. His hands continue to shuffle through the eerie pile, almost out of control, as he takes in page after page of impossible titles.

Okay, thinks George. *This isn't weird. This isn't creepy at all. Hell, this is the most normal thing I've seen tonight.*

Whatever the dude's interested in, he isn't about to judge him for it—he's fine not having anything to do with it. He's just starting to back away from the desk when a sound from the back room causes him to jump. A few papers flutter to the ground, and he curses as he scrambles to pick them up. He doesn't need the guy to know he was looking through his things. The last thing he needs is to be freaking cursed or something, who *knows* what curses the dude has up his sleeve—

His eyes catch on the paper in his hands, something in his brain flickers on like a struck match. This is one of those pages with those intricate drawings; a large circle rests in the center of the page, sketched out in pen. Unusual symbols border the circle, and in the center, there is a large star, which he's seen enough horror movies to recognize. It is a pentagram: a witch's symbol.

CONTRACTING A DEMON, reads this page in bold print.

Before his heart has the chance to jump out his throat and start tap-dancing on the counter, the door opens again. George doesn't think, he doesn't even realize what he's doing; he leaps away from the counter like it's on fire, shoving both hands in his pockets.

The bookstore owner emerges first, followed by George's trio of friends. George takes a second to assess them; Josh, Matt, and Alex all look normal. There's no blood dripping from their eyes or horns growing places horns definitely shouldn't be growing from. Whatever the guy's into, he hasn't done anything to his friends.

"Hey," he says in a voice that's probably too loud. "I was waiting for you guys!"

"Yeah?" The bookstore owner gives him a strange look. George feels something in his stomach shrivel. He knows— oh, he definitely knows. That, or George is acting really shifty for no reason, which is even *more* suspicious.

"Soto, you sure you don't have to go take a leak?" Matt asks, leaning against the doorframe. "You look like it."

"Nah, he always looks like that," slurs Josh. "C'mon, let's go home now."

"Good plan," Alex agrees. They file out from behind the counter and start beelining towards the door, to George—and the bookstore owner's—obvious relief. Thanks are called over their shoulders, and the owner waves back at them with a tired smirk on his face. George makes sure to wave too, even as he's the last one out the door.

He feels sure the store owner can hear his heart pounding in his chest, even once he's all the way down the street. Only when the bookstore is out of sight does he allow his breathing to go uneven. It's the freakiness of those papers, plus the one burning a hole in his pocket. It's the way his heart is pounding with the realization that he's just stolen something—he's never stolen anything in his life. It's the knowledge that there are people who actually *believe* in shit like this, and all that stuff was smack in the middle of an otherwise-normal bookshop.

George doesn't realize he's laughing until he stumbles against the wall, breathless. His friends are giving him weird looks, but he can't bring himself to care.

"Aww, hell," says Alex. "You drank more than all of us put together."

Wordlessly, George withdraws his hand from his pocket. The paper comes with it, crumpled but otherwise in fine shape. He looks down at it and cracks up all over again.

Matt is the one to pry the paper from his hands. He peers at it closer than necessary, brows furrowing up in bafflement, before understanding dawns over his face. "No way. You didn't take this from that guy!"

"I did," confesses George through giggles. "I did!"

"What the hell is this?"

Josh plucks it from Matt's fingers. "Demon summoning," he says, and then blinks like he can't believe what he's just read. "What the hell?"

"It's crazy, that's what it is. Dude had papers like that all over the place. He's a total nut."

Alex is the one to take the paper next, and he skims over it faster than any drunken man should be capable of. He's the one who looks most disturbed as he hands it back to George; his eyes flicker over his shoulder, like he's expecting a demon or the bookshop owner to be standing right behind them.

"You shouldn't have taken that, Soto. You should give it back."

"Tonight? Nooo. No way, not in hell. I wouldn't go back to that creep shop if you paid me." To emphasize his point, George starts strolling down the sidewalk again. After a moment of hesitation, his friends follow.

"The guy was nice, though," says Josh. "Had a nice bathroom."

"He probably summons ghosts in it. Casper was watching you piss," Matt snorts, and George has to be urged along when he starts giggling all over again.

Somehow they make it back to George's apartment before two in the morning, and they all crash in the living room in various states of intoxication. It's a familiar scene, one that's played out hundreds of times, throughout their respective apartments. (When Matt and Josh were roommates, it was funny, but since Matt moved in with his girlfriend Lila, she hasn't appreciated it.) Josh winds up sprawled over the couch, half his body hanging over the side. Alex is slumped on the floor, head pillowed against George's sneakers. Matt always ends up passing out anywhere he can comfortably lay down. Tonight he's under the table.

Why George finds himself curled up with a blanket on the floor even though he has his own bed in the next room, he has no clue. He tells himself he's too much of a friend to leave these idiots alone.

"Jesus," he mutters. "I'm gonna be so freakin' hungover tomorrow. I might die."

"If I'm not dead, just kill me," Alex deadpans. This sends Josh into a fit of giggling, which is only shut up by his friend swinging a pillow at his head. "Go to sleep, O'Brien."

"I am sleeping," Josh says, and makes a clumsy swing back at Alex. He misses by a mile.

George pillows his head in his arms, turning his back on the duo. He was supposed to have work tomorrow, but he already called in a day off (which is probably why Sawyer had it in for him all afternoon). Tomorrow, he can expect a blissful day of doing nothing, and he's never been happier for it.

Matt's eyes peer out at him from under the table, drowsy and half lidded. He looks like he's going to drop off any minute; George doesn't realize he's even awake enough to speak until a soft voice drifts out from the darkness. "You gonna do it, you think?"

George opens his eyes, blinking at Matt.

"The paper. Summon a demon." He can hear the smile in Matt's voice. "Could be fun."

"Like hell'm I doing that." George snorts. "What do I wanna start vomiting pea soup and spinning my head around for? No thanks, I'm good."

"I dare you to," Matt mutters. "Film it. We can all laugh at it later."

"You're crazy."

"Yeah. A little bit. Someone has to keep your life exciting."

George rolls his eyes before closing them once more, exhaling a loud sigh to make it clear he's no longer listening. Matt's always been the type of person to let his ideas run wild; what's worse, his enthusiasm tends to be infectious. It is very hard to say "no" to Matt. He hears his friend chuckling in the darkness and feels a hand ruffle his hair. He's sleepy enough that he allows it.

"Happy birthday, George," Matt whispers, and George huffs a soft laugh.

"Thanks, buddy," he mumbles. "It's been a good one."

WHEN GEORGE WAKES up the next morning, his hangover is somehow worse than he expected it to be.

Alex is already slumped over the table when George stumbles into the kitchen. He's nursing a cup of coffee in his hands, but his face is pressed against the tabletop. He doesn't look conscious. George pokes his shoulder as he walks past and gets no reply.

"I was gonna check for a pulse," Matt says from the other side of the kitchen, where he's got George's sunglasses perched on his face and is pouring Cheerios into a coffee cup with clumsy hands. "He didn't move, but said he'd disembowel me if I tried."

"Morning, Allie!" George chimes with over-the-top cheeriness, despite the physical pain it causes him. Alex lets out a strained noise, like a whimper. His forehead slams down on the table with a thud.

George glances over at Matt (eating dry Cheerios with his fingers out of a porcelain mug) and pulls a bowl from one of the top shelves. He doesn't offer it to him; instead, he steals the box and pours himself his own breakfast. Matt can do what he wants. "Who the hell is using my shower?"

"You *know* who," Alex grumbles. "Asshole."

Sure enough, it's only a few minutes before Josh emerges from a cloud of steam in George's bathroom. With a towel wrapped around his waist, he strolls into the kitchen and steals Alex's coffee right from his hands. "Morning, guys!" he chirps, greeting them with a bright grin that makes George's head pound even worse.

"Josh, I love you, and you know I appreciate your biceps," George says, "but I am currently seeing more of your body than I ever wanted to see. Get the hell out of my kitchen, and put some pants on."

Matt mutters a "thank you" as Josh, humbled, exits the kitchen in search of pants. He takes Alex's coffee with him.

Anyone who knows the first thing about George Soto knows he loves his friends. He's committed to them to a fault; he'd fight for them, die for them, without stopping to take a breath. He'd gladly give them the shirt off his back if he could, and knows they'd do the same for him. He appreciates his friends and enjoys almost every minute he spends with them.

Almost every minute. Hungover on the day after his birthday with his house full of too-loud guys is not one of these minutes.

Fortunately for George, they're all easy to kick out. Alex has to work in a few hours anyway (poor bastard) and Josh has his own things to do. Matt seems like he'd be content to laze around for the rest of the day on George's couch, (and has been known to do so in the past), but another threat to call Lila to come get him sends him scurrying out the door.

Left alone at last, George does what he's wanted to do since he woke up: he strips down, flops into bed, and passes out.

When he wakes up, it's well past noon, and the sunlight streaming through his shades is no longer enough to make him want to cry. He sits up, groaning at the creaking of his bones and looks around with bleary eyes. It doesn't seem like they trashed his apartment last night, thank God. His room remains untouched from how he left it yesterday morning. There's a tan lump on his dresser that's moving a bit, which tells him the cat has let herself into his room and fallen asleep, as per usual.

He probably needs to feed her—and himself, too.

"Come on, Dora, get your lazy butt up," he mutters, dragging himself out of bed. Predictably, the cat doesn't move.

He takes two steps towards the door before he trips and winds up sprawled on his carpet. The floor isn't half as inviting as the bed, so he drags himself up with a groan before leaning over to look at what's trying to kill him this time. His jeans, discarded before he hopped into bed, are tangled around his legs and keeping him rooted to the floor.

George murmurs a number of creative curses as he fights to untangle himself. His bedroom floor is littered with discarded clothes, papers, and other things he couldn't try to name. He's lucky he landed on the floor, and not something that would actually hurt.

He's just got his pants away from him when he hears the sound of paper crinkling. His curiosity piques; it only takes digging in the jean pockets for a moment before he pulls out a crumpled piece of paper.

His heart sinks. He'd forgotten about the creepy-as-hell bookstore from last night. Somewhere between finding their way back to the apartment and the hangover, it completely slipped his mind. Even as the memory of Matt's dare comes floating back to him, George realizes there's no way he can bring back this paper without looking like a creeper.

He really doesn't want to have a conversation with the bookstore owner about whatever occult stuff he might be into. It's none of George's business, and he's never had an interest in stuff like that. The guy can do his own thing—

George doesn't want to be involved. The sane thing to do, he knows, would be to throw the paper away.

He pulls himself to his feet with the intent to do just that and makes it halfway to the kitchen before he stops. Holding the paper up to the light again, he scrutinizes the strange circle and allows his eyes to scan over the directions written above it.

The ritual really isn't that complicated. Draw a circle, scribble down the runes, draw the star thingy in the middle, provide an "offering," and then read out a short paragraph in a language George can't understand. The offering is the most disturbing part; the paper makes sure to specify that nothing less than blood will work for this ceremony.

It's absurd in the best way. The entire sheet reads like a well-thought-out practical joke and touches upon all of George's favorite horror movie clichés: pentagrams, ritualistic chanting, and blood offerings. This is freaking hilarious, and he can see why Matt thought it would be such a great dare last night.

George's mind drifts back to his friend's words, and he glances from his phone to the paper again.

It's an awful idea. He recognizes that, and acknowledges it goes against every pre-conceived resolution not to get involved in any of this spooky shit.

But damn, wouldn't it be a *hilarious* prank?

He could record himself doing the bogus ritual. Then, with the help of a little video editing magic, he could make it look like an actual demon appeared and watch Matt freak out when he shows it to him. He could get all of his friends with this; hell, even Sawyer might buy it, if George makes the special effects look good. It would be just like a movie, and a joke that would have George rolling on the floor.

George Soto loves a good joke. God knows he's had *way* worse ideas than this one.

"What the hell," he says out loud, and goes to search for some chalk.

SKETCHING THE CIRCLE takes longer than expected. He creates one outer ring and one inner ring. That's the easy part. The real labor comes when he has to create the sigils. There are over a dozen scattered all around the edges of the circle, each one an intricate series of lines and twists. He fights to keep his hand steady, using the sketch on paper as reference as he draws out every last symbol. By the time he's done, his wrist aches, and he hasn't even gotten to the pentagram yet.

By the time the pentagram is finished, George is exhausted. After scrounging up some candles and placing them around the circle, he'll admit the effect looks cool, but can't help wondering if this was such a great idea after all. This seems like a lot of effort for a stupid prank. Then he remembers some of the things he's pulled off in the past, such as the zebra prank or the one on Josh's birthday, and he realizes this isn't half as much work.

With renewed enthusiasm, he switches to his phone and starts recording. Now that the ambiance has been set, the real ritual can begin, and he wants to get every moment of it on film.

"Matt, I hope you appreciate this, because I'm doing it for you. This was your dare. This is your fault." George points at the camera, then holds up a sewing pin. "The ritual thing said you had to make a blood offering, right? So, I'm going to make a blood offering. This is absolutely how people get possessed in horror flicks, I know, so if I start foaming at the mouth and levitating, something's probably gone to hell. Literally."

He sets his phone up to record him and finally moves into the circle. He stands in the center of the circle, right in the heart of the pentagram, and holds up his index finger.

The pin hurts more than expected, but it's a brief sting. He pushes just enough to draw blood before pulling it away and watches crimson liquid bloom on the tip of his finger.

Blood drips to form a small spot in the center of the circle. Each drop makes the puddle grow a bit bigger. Looking at it makes George feel queasy. Hastily, he turns to the next step of the ritual.

The last step, he reminds himself, and could almost sigh in relief. Holding up the paper, he narrows his eyes at the unfamiliar Latin and begins to read aloud.

> *"Ego adsum si vocare te*
> *voluntatem mea, serve meus, ad causam*
> *ego sto do tibi ius*
> *ego conjuro te*
> *factum est."*

At first, nothing happens.

There is a moment of silence, heavy with a tense anticipation George hadn't even realized he felt. It's like he expects something to happen, while at the same time hoping and praying it *won't*. As the seconds stretch on, filled with nothing but the sound of his own heartbeat, George's anxiety begins to mellow out.

Of *course* nothing happened. He slowly steps backward out of the circle, fighting the urge to chuckle to himself. What did he *think* the ritual would do?

He thought it would do nothing, but its purpose was to summon a demon—which isn't possible. He worked himself up over nothing! What on earth was he expect—

George gets his only warning when the temperature of the room take a sharp nosedive. The hairs on his arms shoot up as if electrified. At the same time, the air seems to grow *heavier*. In a single second, the room feels like it has been filled with smoke; George finds himself struggling to breathe. He reels around, gripping his throat against the suddenly congested air. His jaw drops.

"What the *hell*," mutters George, shrinking back against the wall.

What stands in the middle of his apartment can best be described as a tornado, but it can't really be described at all. It is a pulsating mass of energy—a black cloud of thick smoke, writhing and churning like the ocean in the middle of a storm. George can see flickers of electricity in the all-consuming blackness, lightning in the midst of dark oblivion.

The very presence leaves his head spinning. He tries to turn, but dizziness gets the better of him and he collapses to his knees. There is a buzzing in his ears that sounds like screaming. An icy hand has his chest in a vice grip and is squeezing hard, pulling him in. He knows what it's trying to do—it wants to get him back in the circle, with that thing.

George digs his fingernails into the wooden floor, bracing himself against the chaos from all sides. The air is pressing down on top of him; he feels like he's underwater and can't come up for air.

His vision is starting to black out around the edges. He prays it's from shock, not from the lack of oxygen, and not because he's about to die at the hands of this thing.

The last thing he hears before he falls unconscious is a voice, deep as thunder and rough as gravel under the wheel of a steamroller. It echoes around him, piercing the hollowest corners of his mind, and maybe it's this that finally knocks him out.

"What the *fuck* are you trying to do?"

Chapter Two

WHEN GEORGE OPENS his eyes, it's to a puddle of his own drool pooling beneath his face.

He pulls himself off of the floor with slow movements, keenly aware of the pounding in his head. He is careful not to look behind him; instead he keeps his eyes trained on the wall in front of him, his own shadow solid against the candle flame.

The air still feels heavy, but it is no longer suffocating. He can feel an electric current coursing through the room; it shocks him a bit every time he tries to focus on it. A dull ache lingers in his chest, sort of like recovering from a punch, but when he tries to rub it, he finds no pain on his skin. The ache is coming from *inside* his body, and that doesn't disturb him half as much as it should. It is far from the craziest thing happening right now.

There is a demon in his living room. Right behind him.

George almost has himself convinced he's prepared for what he'll see as he turns around. He isn't.

"Holy shit," he mutters, kind of wishing he could pass out again. "Holy—holy *shit.*"

The mass of black demonic hellbeast is still there. It hasn't gone away, like George really hoped it would. If anything, it has to have gotten even bigger since George passed out. Now it's straining at the boundaries of the circle like it's eager to bust through. George takes weak comfort in the fact that the circle seems to be the only thing keeping it contained.

Still. Giant pulsing *demon thing* in his apartment.

His landlady is gonna murder him.

"Holy shit," George says again, in both shock and dismay.

An invisible shockwave courses through the air. It's strong enough that George can feel it running over his skin, but the contents of his apartment remain undisturbed. He tenses at the feeling of energy cresting over his body like a wave. In front of him, the mass of shadow ripples.

"Great," snarls the voice of the demon. "I've been summoned by an idiot."

Now, he may have just screwed with a whole lot of occult stuff without the first clue what he's doing, but George still has his pride. "Wow. Okay, well, at least I've got a freakin' body."

The demon seems to take stock of itself—as much as a writhing mass of smoke can, anyway—and shudders with disdain. "I *had* a body," it snarls, voice rumbling through the room like an earthquake tremor. "Until you yanked me out of it and dragged my ass here. Feel like telling me why you did that?"

George blinks, disoriented. It's probably too late to tell the demon this was all a prank *now*.

"I, umm—I needed a reason?"

For a second, the demon is silent. George winces.

"Great," it finally growls. "I've actually been summoned by a dumbass with no clue what the fuck he's doing."

"Wow, real nice!" exclaims George, indignant. It occurs to him too late that back-sassing the demon in his house is probably not a great idea, but it isn't like he can take it back. If he's going to get killed, he's already dug his own grave. What's the harm of shoveling deeper?

The demon shifts, and George gets the impression that if a mass of smoke could cross its arms, that's what it would be doing.

"Am I wrong?"

"Nah." George might be an idiot, but he's an honest one. "I have no idea what I'm doing. Would you be mad if I told you this was all supposed to be a joke?"

"A joke?" Another tremor courses through the apartment, and George's stomach drops. Now the demon is *definitely* mad. "You summoned me here for a damn *joke?*"

It takes all of George's willpower not to dart into the kitchen and hide in a cabinet. "You know, it seemed like a real riot at the time?"

The pictures on his walls shake. George shrinks closer to the ground, holding up his hands. "Oooh-kay, okay, this is *fine*. We're good. Everything's good. We can figure this out."

How the hell *can* they figure this out? He's got a demon in his apartment, no clue what to do with it, and it's getting angrier with every passing second. George is at a loss. The only thing he can think to do is what he always does—he keeps talking. "I gotta admit, you're not being too clear with me here. You're asking me for stuff, not saying what, you're probably leaving scorch marks on my ceiling—or stains, hell, I don't know what you're made of. So—so why don't you just tell me? What do you want me to do?"

The demon considers this for a moment. "You could shut up, that'd be nice."

"Fine," George muttered, rolling his eyes. Figures he would wind up summoning a grumpy-ass demon, instead of Casper the Friendly Ghost. "What do you want to do?"

"I don't *wanna* do anything," says the demon, sounding fantastically put-upon. "You're supposed to tell me to do something, and I do it. You made a blood contract to get me here, that's sort of how this works."

George's mind races to keep up with the conversation, but he still finds himself floundering. His mind flashes back to the title of the ritual—*Contracting A Demon*, not just summoning. Apparently, contracting is a lot more complicated. Has he just made a deal with the devil without even realizing it? "Wait a minute—you're telling me you gotta do whatever I say?"

"Until the contract is fulfilled, yes." The demon sounds pained.

"What happens when the contract's up?"

"Let's just say you're not my problem anymore. You made the deal already, you should have known what you're getting into."

And *there* it is. George had no clue what he was getting into, which was how he ended up in this mess in the first place. George grimaces; he can tell the demon realizes exactly how dumb he is. Maybe he's still clinging to the desperate hope that he's been summoned by a competent person, just like George is to the hope that this *isn't actually happening*.

"Are we gonna set the terms for this or not? I've got stuff I need to be doing."

"Glad to know I summoned the busiest demon in all of freakin' hell." George rolls his eyes. "Fine. I just... give you a job, you do it?"

"That's how it works."

"Great. Okay, I need—well, yeah, sure," George fumbles. This whole conversation has been him flying by the seat of his pants. He hasn't had the chance to think of anything. He has no clue what he could do with a demon— he doesn't want to hurt anyone, he's not about to use this surly bastard as a joke, and if he doesn't give it something to do he's pretty sure this guy is going to eat him. *Just think, George,* he urges himself. *Anything will work.*

Suddenly, he has it, and he could almost laugh out loud. How didn't he think of it from the beginning?

"Look, my boss is an asshole. He's a total jerk. Completely sadistic. He's brutal to the interns, he hammers us for tiny mistakes, he docks our pay over nothing. If you could... *take care* of him somehow, I'd really appreciate it."

The demon is quiet for a few seconds, leaving George to agonize in the well of his own words. When it finally speaks, there's an undercurrent of incredulity to its voice. "You want me to kill the guy? You're asking me to kill him."

"What? No, whoa, *no!*" George almost falls over his own feet. "That's not what's happening here!"

"What the fuck do you think 'take care of him' means?"

Okay, bad choice of phrasing there. Definitely bad. Demons take things (especially violence) literally; George notes this for later reference.

"Just... scare the hell out of him. I don't care what you gotta do, but get in there and scare all the asshole right out of him. I mean, look at you—" George gestures to the demon's eldritch appearance, and the smoky mass writhes as if pleased. "Not like it's gonna be hard."

A thousand cracks of lightning flash in front of George's eyes. The demon's entire mass seems to ripple; it's dizzying to watch. That old familiar lightheadedness begins to creep back, and George has to close his eyes until he can catch his equilibrium again.

The demon has no sympathy for him. It has what it came here for. "We got a deal?"

"Yeah." George takes a deep breath and opens his eyes, nodding. "Guess it is a deal. What, do I shake your hand or something?"

"Why not?"

Before George can start explaining the concept of a joke to his new best friend, something shifts. He has no clue what's happening at first, only that the mass in front of him is rippling. The sight makes his vision blur. It takes a few seconds for his eyes to focus again, and when they do, he is shocked to realize the massive demon has vanished. What's left behind is the last thing George could have expected.

He doesn't know *what's* standing in front of him. All George knows is that he's summoned a demon straight off the cover of *Fitness* magazine. The guy standing in front of him is tall and well-built, all tawny skin stretched over developed muscle. Dark hair shaved short accentuates his strong jaw. He stands with easy confidence, broad shoulders straight and set forward as if ready for a challenge. His lack of a shirt shows off not only his physique, but it's decorations as well. Winding black tattoos ink his arms and torso, complex patterns that must have meanings George can't decode. His eyes are full black, sharp and wry as they study George from beneath heavy lids. Even his lips are striking, jutting out in a pout that looks like it belongs on an ancient statue.

He exudes the air of a football player or boxer. Freaky powers aside, George realizes the demon could probably crush him anyway; while he doesn't tower over the rest of the room, there is power in his broad frame that makes him seem invincible.

It takes George's awestruck brain a few seconds to realize *this* is his demon.

"Whoa," he squeaks, face flaming with heat like a radiator. "*That's* your human form?"

The demon raises one strong eyebrow. "What, you don't like it? I can be a little old lady, too, or a tiny kid. If you want dentures and a metal hip—"

"*No*, no no—I like it." George comes close to choking on his own tongue. "It's great."

Those *abs*. He could slice his hands open on those abs, but he doesn't give a shit because he wants to touch them anyway. He'd pay money to get within a few *feet* of those abs. They're currently standing in his living room in all their ripped, glistening glory.

The demon is *shining*. Is he wearing body oil? George thinks he is. He's still way too hungover to handle this.

The demon takes a step towards the barrier of the circle. He glances at his feet pointedly, and it takes George a moment to realize what he's looking for. Maybe it's the spell of those abs, or those biceps, or that face, but he doesn't think twice before dragging his foot through the chalk lines.

The barrier smudges, and as easily as that it's broken. George can feel the energy dissipating like lightning on the wind. He shudders; the demon's lips twitch.

"My name is Valac. You can call me Jack," the demon says, thrusting a hand forward. George only hesitates for a second before taking it.

"George Soto," he says. "Pleasure doing business with you."

THE NEXT DAY is so normal that it's almost easy for George to convince himself it was just a dream.

The chalk, he finds, won't wash out of his floors unless he breaks his back scrubbing, so he elects to leave it there overnight. Once the deal was made, Jack was quick to vanish, leaving the room blissfully empty without his presence. George misses his face, but that's about it. He leaves the circle right where it is and doesn't see another sign of Jack for the rest of the night.

That morning he hauls himself out of bed, gets dressed, and leaves the house the same way he does every morning. He almost forgets his keys (as usual), grabs a cup of coffee from the shop at the corner of his street (as usual), and responds to whatever weird texts his friends sent him overnight (as usual). By the time he gets to work, everything is so ordinary that all thoughts of demon-summonings-which-feel-like-dreams are easily pushed from his mind.

Then Sawyer happens.

Sawyer *happens* every day, to the dismay of everyone unfortunate enough to work under him. Today, however, Sawyer seems determined to *happen* even more than usual.

"Brewer, I asked you for a copy of the *Andrews* report, not the *Anderson* report. If you're so incompetent that you can't read, why are you working at a law firm instead of at McDonald's?"

McDonald's employees *can* read, George wants to say, and they can probably write a hell of a lot better than Sawyer's chicken scratch. He holds his tongue. The last thing he wants is to put a target on his back when Sawyer's already in a foul mood. He's spent the whole morning antagonizing Brewer, and the poor intern looks ready to swan dive down the elevator shaft just to get away from him.

"Geraldson, get me a coffee. If it's cold by the time you get back, you have coffee detail for the rest of the week. Am I talking to a wall? When I give an order, you jump!" Sawyer claps his hands for emphasis. Geraldson jumps to his feet and scurries out of the room. With him gone, Sawyer rounds on the rest of the office. "As for the rest of you, we *need* to increase our billable hours! We have a quota of cases to meet by the end of the month, and at the rate you slouches work, we won't get close. Every man has to pull his load and more. Let's move, people!"

That's Sawyer's motto, *Let's Move, People*—as if that's actually going to spur anyone to work faster. George can't speak for anybody else but having someone scream in his ear usually makes him work slower, not faster, no matter what Sawyer's twisted "colleague relations" seminars must have taught him. Day in, day out, that's all anyone in the office ever heard—Sawyer's bellowing voice, urging them to work harder. George sometimes hears Sawyer in his nightmares.

One day George is gonna shove all of his *Let's Move, People's* up his ass, along with his resignation letter. (That will be the day he moves to Cuba, changes his identity, and resigns himself to living in shame for the rest of his life. Still, a guy can dream.)

When he first joined the company, George was fresh out of college and desperate for a steady paycheck. Finding work at the most prominent law firm in town seemed like his big break, even if he'd only be an office grunt. He could have never anticipated having to deal with a boss who didn't know the meaning of an indoor voice. To be fair, back then, Sawyer hadn't been half as much of a drill sergeant. *It was the divorce that did him in*, George thinks; the divorce, the kidney stones, and losing his prized rose bushes to a rogue pair of his neighbor's hedge clippers.

A run of bad luck was apparently enough to turn Sawyer into every employee's worst nightmare. He started out a halfway decent boss. He got worse.

The only thing that keeps George coming back to this office every day is the need for a consistent paycheck. Otherwise George would have been out of here months ago, and not looked back once.

All he can do until his glorious day of resignation comes is to keep his head down, do his job, and not kill his boss in the meantime. One day this will all be worth it, and he'll know what the hell it was he spent so long working towards in the first place.

He narrows his eyes on his computer screen, trying to block Sawyer out. It's not easy.

"Hey, Gomez," George says as he notices his coworker making his way towards the coffee machine. "Can you get me one too? You're my guy, you know how I like it!"

Gomez nods, and George flashes him an exaggerated grin. He's appeased by the small quirk of the younger man's lips as he turns to the Styrofoam cups. There's not a lot of joy in this office, but George knows how important it is to keep spirits up. If he can do anything to alleviate the tension Sawyer brings to the workplace, hell, he considers that as much his job as reviewing paperwork.

He's just turning back to his screen when he hears a sharp hissing noise, followed by a yelp from Gomez. His head shoots up in time to see his coworker stumbling back from the machine. A thick cloud of black smoke is spewing out of it, painting the air in the kitchen a sick ashy color. Gomez makes his retreat, putting as much distance between himself and the coffee machine as possible as it continues spewing blackness.

George's eyes linger on the smoke as it dissipates in the air, and he swears he catches a tiny flash of electricity.

"What just happened?" demands Sawyer, striding over to the coffee maker. The last of the smoke is evaporating as he gets there, and he peers at the machine with over-the-top suspicion. "Gomez, tell me you didn't just break this machine."

"No, sir," Gomez answers promptly. "It just *did* that, I only pressed a button, I don't know what—"

"Oh, you know that broken office equipment will come out of your paycheck. You'd better hope this thing still works," Sawyer declares, shoving an empty coffee mug beneath the machine and pressing one of the buttons. George holds his breath, waiting—for what, he isn't sure. Maybe the coffee maker will blow up. Maybe Sawyer will go flying out the window. Maybe his hair will catch on fire, or Jack in all his inky glory will materialize in the middle of the office and make Sawyer shit his pants.

Nothing happens. The machine releases a steady stream of coffee into Sawyer's cup.

Gomez heaves a sigh of relief as he scurries back into his seat. He casts George an apologetic look. George shrugs his shoulders. He's disappointed, but not because he didn't get his coffee. For a split second, he'd been sure his wish upon a demon had come true. (Could it really be possible he only imagined Jack?)

"You type like a two-year-old, Carroll," says Sawyer, beginning his rounds of the office once again. "You have more fingers than your two index ones. Learn to use them!"

George tenses as his boss passes behind him. To his relief, Sawyer doesn't stop. "If you call this a case review, Larsen, you deserve to get sued."

Sawyer is passing in front of him when George feels it— a chill running across his skin and making his hair stand on end, not unlike a brief charge of electricity.

"Samuels, I have no clue what you're typing, but never in my life have I seen more incompetent review work. If I took this to the client now, you would be fired so quickly your head would be spinning. You do *not* deserve to work in this office—"

And just like that, Sawyer's coffee mug shatters.

Oh, thinks George as boiling liquid spills everywhere, especially all over Sawyer's shirt. He wasn't imagining things after all.

Sawyer's reaction is immediate and appropriate: a lot of yelling, a lot of jumping around, and a hell of a lot of cursing.

It stands as testament to Sawyer's popularity in the office that no one tries to help him, or even reacts aside from gaping at the shattered porcelain on the floor. There is a large coffee stain on the hideous beige carpeting; George thinks it's an improvement. When Sawyer runs straight into a desk and nearly winds up taking out an entire computer, someone laughs out loud.

"Get me a towel!" Sawyer is screaming. "A towel, now!"

Brewer finally tosses Sawyer a towel, and he is quick to wipe as much of the scalding liquid from his chest as possible. Once he's able to collect himself again, he draws himself up to his full height—ignorant of, or just not caring about the brown liquid drenching his shirt.

For a moment, the office holds its collective breath. No one knows what Sawyer's next move will be, but they all know it's going to be something bad. Slowly, Sawyer turns until his gaze lands on Gomez.

"What," he enunciates, "in *hell* did you do to my coffee mug?"

Poor Gomez has just been tossed in the deep end without a life vest.

"What? Nothing, sir, I didn't do anything!"

"Well, someone obviously did *something!* Mugs don't just explode just like that!"

"Maybe the coffee was too hot," someone pipes up, and Sawyer rounds on them next.

"Too hot? Too hot! Well, who the hell made it too hot? That machine barely makes warm coffee as it is! If it was hot enough to explode an entire cup, then I would have no skin on my chest right now! Since it wasn't the liquid, someone clearly *sabotaged* the mug, and so help me if no one confesses now I'll find out who—"

George notices when the printers start to go haywire, only because they drown out Sawyer's hollering. The wails pierce the office, sirens screeching an invisible emergency. It's shrill enough to send those closest to the printers covering their ears and diving out of the way. The printer's lights are flashing wildly, and no one wants a giant hunk of metal to go in the way of Sawyer's coffee cup. George takes a step back from the nearest printer, eyes darting around the room in mute amazement. Sawyer's mouth is hanging open; he looks dumbstruck, but it's an improvement from his usual red-faced rage.

"What's going on?" he mouths. "What's happening—"

"Let's move, people!" the intercom suddenly blares over the printers' wailing. "Get your asses into gear! We don't have all day! Let's work!"

It's a perfect imitation of Sawyer's voice. If the man wasn't standing in front of him, George would even say it was Sawyer, spewing his abuse throughout the entire building. "You useless pieces of shit couldn't type if your lives depended on it! When you get fired for laziness and wind up dishing out fast food, maybe you'll wish you learned how to actually work!"

"What the hell is going on?" Sawyer hollers over the din. As if in reply, the computers go as well. Every screen shorts out, flashing a luminescent white, before they begin to hiss and rattle. Violent beeps sound from each desk; distorted pictures of Sawyer fill the screen, zooming in on his face and twisting to the point of unrecognizability. They only last for a second a piece, a nightmarish slideshow of their boss' face.

It's only a few pictures in, however, before other images get thrown into the mix: gory landscapes of torture scenes, oozing wounds, and nightmare images that make George have to turn away to save his suddenly revolting stomach.

This is the last straw. Papers fly from desks as Sawyer sprints through the office, past broken porcelain and rioting technology. He doesn't leave the din behind him; it seems to follow him all the way to the elevators, each screech intensifying the harder he presses the button.

George can't blame him for getting the hell out of here. Sawyer's no idiot—this is the time to leave and leave fast. He can't say he's sorry to see his boss go as the elevator doors open and Sawyer flings himself inside.

Then George's eyes fix on the lone figure standing inside the elevator. He's leaning with his back to the wall, pose so relaxed that he is out of place in the office's chaos. Maybe it is this very casual air that makes him almost invisible. He's dressed plainly, a dark suit over a gray shirt—smart, flattering, but not notable. A hat is lowered over his eyes.

He tilts his head up just enough for George to catch a glimpse of his face beneath the hat's rim, and he feels his heart leap in his chest. Black eyes catch his, and wink.

The door closes to a cowering Sawyer in one corner and Jack's relaxed smirk in the other.

When they open again in the lobby, only one person is found in the elevator: Rob Sawyer, fifth-floor supervisor, is unconscious, naked, and covered in sharpie marks. Crude drawings litter the bare skin of his face, chest, and legs; more intricate drawings, almost like symbols, are scattered in various other places. No one can identify these symbols, nor can they pinpoint the cause of the various scratches Sawyer seems to be covered in, red and swollen but not enough to break the skin. Sawyer's clothes are nowhere to be found; neither is the elevator's other occupant, who may never have been there to begin with.

Sawyer is taken to the hospital, where doctors declare him in perfect health (though he won't stop rambling about offices going berserk and being cornered by a man with black eyes).

Sawyer's clothing is found in the fountain outside the building later that day. Some poor intern is given the thankless task of hauling the drenched articles out and laying them to dry, only to discover they've been shredded to the point of uselessness. No one has any good explanation, though by the end of shift everyone is scrambling to come up with the most outlandish one they can think of. Someone put LSD in the coffee; the elevator is haunted; Sawyer was cursed by somebody with a grudge (his ex-wife seems to be the going theory); or maybe karma is just a bitch.

No one has any idea what really happened (except for George Soto).

When Sawyer quits the next day, not a soul in the office sheds a tear.

THOUGH GEORGE ISN'T actually sure Jack will show his face again, he figures it's best to be prepared. He doesn't change into his pajamas that night. He leaves his pants on—a rare thing for an evening alone—orders pizza and settles down on the couch to watch a movie.

He's just closed the door on the pizza guy when the air behind him suddenly grows heavier. George knows what to expect before he turns around to find Jack lounging with casual grace at the end of his couch.

"Hey," he greets, meeting the demon with a wide grin. "Jack, buddy! I wondered if you were gonna show up!"

"I did what you asked," Jack says. "The contract's up."

"Yeah, yeah, I know." George waves a hand, nodding as he carries the pizza over to the couch. "You came at a good time. Pizza's still hot. I've also got beer. You want beer? Can you drink beer? I dunno, it's shitty beer, but it's cheap and alcoholic, so my two favorite things. I'll go get it. Sit down. Kick off your shoes or something."

Jack looks very stiff, any easiness having faded from his posture. Now he's lingering at the end of the couch like he doesn't know what to do, and it's enough to make George uncomfortable in sympathy. He gestures to the couch and the pizza. "Hey. Don't stand there like a statue. What, are you afraid my mom's gonna come out and yell at us for tracking dirt on the floor? Make yourself at home."

Jack doesn't speak until George is in the kitchen, head buried in the fridge as he scrounges for his six-pack of beer. "What the hell are you doing, George?"

"What's it seem like I'm doing? Looking for something to drink."

"No—" Jack's voice is rough, but also stilted. *"This.* You're treating me like... some sort of guest."

George pops out of the fridge, six-pack clutched in his hand. He takes a moment to peer out the kitchen doorway at Jack, who has taken an uneasy seat on the couch. It couldn't be more obvious that he's uncomfortable. He has no clue what George is doing, and for some reason, that makes George smirk. "No, I'm treating you like a friend. If you're going to take care of my boss in the most awesome, freaky-as-shit way possible, pop into my apartment uninvited, and drink my beer, you're a friend. That's how it works."

Jack's brow furrows. "I'm not your friend. I'm a demon. You contracted me."

"Sure," accepts George easily as he settles down on the other side of the couch, pulling out a beer and offering it to Jack. "I didn't have any demon friends before, though—didn't even know you guys existed. I figure we may as well get to know each other."

This makes Jack scoff. The sound is rougher than sandpaper. George would kill to hear it on a loop forever. It's one of *those* laughs that remain in your head after you hear it once, playing over and over again. He finds himself resolved to draw it out of Jack once more, no matter how many lame jokes he has to tell.

"You wanna know me?"

Short answer: yes. Jack in his human form is a lot less terrifying than as a writhing mass of smoke. George has no experience with demons, but he does know people. Getting along with others is familiar territory for him. Making new friends is something he's good at. He's always had a silver tongue, a way of endearing himself, turning strangers into friends. Maneuvering this ability to coax people out of their shells and figure them out—these are all areas where George excels.

The truth is, now that he's no longer terrified, he's *curious* about Jack. He wants to learn about his life. George wants to know everything about Jack—his job, his life, his abilities—the feeling of those strong lips, whether his hair is soft or coarse, if his abs are really as solid as they look.... George wants to know a *lot* about Jack.

"Heck yeah," he says simply.

Jack looks confused for a moment longer before he shifts on the couch, offering an incredulous sigh. "What do you wanna know?"

George's grin widens.

The rest of that night is spent the same way George would spend any night with a friend. He and Jack drink beer and eat pizza, rag on the shitty special effects in whatever movie they're watching, mock the characters, and talk about whatever topics pop into their heads. Granted, George is asking most of the questions. Jack doesn't talk much; he's blunt with his answers, but he doesn't avoid questions and he has a sardonic sense of humor that isn't laugh-out-loud, but George finds he can't get enough of all the same. He ends up learning more about the demon world than he ever thought he would know, but he still feels like he hasn't learned even a quarter of Jack's real life.

"Hang on a minute—you can't shapeshift? What about the whole smoke-to-human thing?"

Jack's sharp edges have been dulled by the beer and prolonged exposure to George. Instead of looking annoyed, he just shrugs. "I've got forms. I can turn into a few different types of human, a wolf, and some sort of freaky thing that breathes fire. Not a dragon—like, a deer with a bull's head, and wings. It's fuckin' weird."

"All demons only have a few forms, or are you just an unlucky bastard?"

Jack smirks at him, and something inside George melts a bit. "Funny. Yeah, we've all got a few forms. Some have the power to shapeshift to anything just because they can, and Kings can turn into whatever the hell they want—but that's going into demon hierarchy, which is way more shit than I'm gonna explain to you right now."

Right now. Does that imply there will be a next time?

"Are you a king?" George leans forward, curious, as Jack snorts.

"Hell no. I'm what's called a Sergeant—which is kind of important, yeah. The rank below that is Private, and any demon without a rank isn't in the hierarchy at all, meaning they have pretty much jack to do with any other world— didn't I just say I wasn't getting into this?"

George shrugs, smirking. "You're talking, I'm just listening."

"I don't usually talk this much. To anyone." Jack frowns down at the beer can in his hands—it's his third, and it's empty. Three beers wouldn't do much for George, but he gets the sense Jack isn't used to human alcohol. If getting him drunk makes him chatty, George resolves to invite Jack over for a beer next time he gets the chance.

"It's okay," he says. "I like hearing you talk."

Jack looks up at him. The flicker of surprise in his dark eyes makes George falter. He forces a grin, trying to pull some of the weight from his previous words. "Besides, I talk too much. We balance each other out!"

Jack chuckles softly but follows it with an inevitable sigh. "I should go."

"What? Where're you going?"

"I told you, George. I've got stuff to do. Things... things I've gotta take care of."

"Oh." George swallows, trying not to feel too disappointed. Glancing at the clock over Jack's shoulder tells him it's getting close to midnight; they've been talking for hours. "Yeah, that's fine. I guess you don't have to worry about the contract anymore, now that's all taken care of."

"Yeah." Jack stands up, brushes off his jeans. He looks uncomfortable once more. "I guess you're right."

"What happens now? Now that it's up?"

"It doesn't matter," Jack answers promptly. George is surprised by the look in his eyes—firm, certain of himself.

It's attractive, to be sure, but he's got no clue where it's coming from. "Now we both go live our damn lives."

"Sure." George can't help the feeling of disappointment that gnaws the inside of his chest. He brushes it aside to offer Jack a wry smile. "Hey, maybe I'll summon you again sometime."

"Don't do that," says Jack. "I really will kill you."

"You won't. You had your chance."

"I mean it, George."

Jack could have left already. He hasn't. Is he as reluctant to leave as George is to see him go?

They stare at each other for a moment. The silence between them seems to say more than either have said all night. George feels breathless, a little dizzy, and finds himself longing to reach out and take Jack's hand just to feel him. He doesn't, of course. If he touches Jack now, he won't want to let him go. He can't look away from those eyes, intense and alive, that stare at him like they want a piece of him.

Finally it's Jack who breaks the spell, turning away. "Bye, George," he says, and fades into the shadows as simply as if he were never there at all.

George stares at the spot where Jack vanishes for a long moment before he smiles to himself. "See you around, Jack."

Chapter Three

"YOU *WHAT?*"

Across the table, the three other men sit in rapt attention. Their eyes are glued on him; their hands are still, thoughts of food and drink having been pushed from their minds completely. George takes perverse pleasure in dragging out the moment as long as possible. He takes a slow sip of beer, watching his friends over the rim of his glass. When he pulls away, he allows himself to smirk.

"Did I stutter? I told you I summoned a demon, so obviously I summoned a freakin' demon."

"You're full of it," Josh dismisses, scoffing. "That, or you're crazy. Who the hell would believe a stupid thing like that?"

George fights the urge to roll his eyes. He expected skepticism, but that doesn't mean it's welcome. It wouldn't be above him to make up some wild story to get under his friends' skin, but he wishes Josh had more faith in him than that. If George wanted to lie, he'd never come up with something so unbelievable without proof to back it up.

"I'm not lying," he insists, tapping the table with his open hand. "His name's Jack. Freakin' Jack, for a demon, can you believe that?"

"No," Alex says loudly. "That's the point."

George exhales in a loud breath, rolling his eyes. "Look, he's not some sort of Tinkerbell 'clap your hands if you believe' thing. I don't need you guys to believe me, I only figured you oughta know. Since this jerk was the one who dared me to do it in the first place."

Matt looks startled as all eyes turn to him. "*Me?*" he exclaims. "When did I do that?"

"Half passed out under my dining room table," George retorts. Matt has to think for a moment before his face clears and he nods.

"Ohh. Right. Well, damn, man, I didn't think you'd actually go through with it."

This time, George really does roll his eyes. "Well, I did, just to show you up. I thought I could turn it into a joke. I had my camera set up and everything, here—" He pulls his phone from his pocket, quickly opening up the video of his first botched (?) summoning. He presses play and turns it to the eager eyes of his friends.

Matt leans forward as he peers at it, only to be nudged aside by Alex. Josh has his chin resting in his palm, gaze following George's movements on the screen. His lips purse, and he gives a low whistle at the intricate design of George's circle. When George pierces his finger, however, he recoils.

"Oh, what the hell, Soto?" Matt exclaims as Alex clamps a shocked hand over his mouth. "That's sick."

"You had to give your blood?" Josh looks incredulous, and a little queasy. "That's crossing a line."

"It's a few drops, I've had nosebleeds a dozen times worse. But watch, see—" George shakes the phone, pushing it closer to his friends' faces. He catches a glimpse of the screen right before it explodes into static, and the video ends abruptly. "Look, you see how it cuts out? Right there. That's when Jack showed up. My phone was completely dead after that."

For a long moment, nobody dares speak. George slips his phone back in his pocket and settles in his seat, crossing his arms. He is gratified by the expressions the other men wear: a mix between alarm, confusion, and fright. It echoes the way George felt the moment he saw Jack for the first time, and he feels a bit of satisfaction to see his friends feeling the same way. It isn't quite revenge, but it's good enough.

"Wow, Soto," Matt says, shaking his head. George thinks he has him for a second, before an impish grin splits his friend's face. "You're really losing your touch. Your editing skills are better than that."

A flicker of relief crosses Josh's face a second before he joins in the laughter. "Yeah, come on. You couldn't have added a few glowing lights? Some shadow people? Even a cartoon ghost. Give us something here."

"I'm not lying! I'm telling you what happened."

"I don't believe it," Josh says.

"Neither do I," agrees Matt, grinning. "George has finally lost his marbles."

"He's gonna go just like Sawyer, down the elevator shaft and into the fountain."

"We'll miss you, buddy!"

In the midst of Matt and Josh's cackling, only Alex looks disturbed. He keeps glancing between the phone and George, as if seeing something that frightens him. After a few seconds, he takes a deep breath and leans in.

"Don't screw around with stuff like that, George. You don't understand it. You could do something bad and not even realize until it's too late."

George blinks, taken aback by his friend's serious tone. Of all people, he hasn't expected Alex to be the one to believe him. Maybe his friend isn't even going that far, but he looks perturbed all the same as he frowns at him. There's a knit in his eyebrows that makes him look younger than he actually is, and he's picking at his nails again—a habit that only rears its head when he's nervous.

"What're you telling me, Alex?"

"I'm saying, stuff like that's dangerous. Even as a joke." Matt and Josh are still laughing and talking over one another, but Alex lowers his voice anyway. "My cousin messed with one of those Ouija boards things at her birthday party, and for weeks afterward crazy stuff kept happening. You don't know what it might do, George. You shouldn't get into this stuff if you don't know what you're messing with."

The entire conversation has taken a turn that's making George uncomfortable for reasons he doesn't want to name. He knows he's in over his head and is flying blind; but being confronted with it so bluntly stings.

Matt gives Alex a sudden clap on the back and the other jolts, springing up once more. The tension is broken; George settles back in his seat, frown playing across his lips.

Alex's words leave a sour taste in his mouth. They linger in his throat like a stone, and he finds himself choking on them for the rest of the night.

JACK'S REAPPEARANCES IN George's apartment have become far less dramatic, but they don't do anything to quell the demon's temper.

"Again?" Jack booms once he's found himself, yet again, trapped in the circle in the middle of George's living room. "You're doing this a-fucking-*gain*?"

"Hey, Jack," greets George, grinning like his birthday has come early. "Handsome as always!"

The mass of black smoke and electricity that is Jack writhes. George can't help but wonder if unsettled demons have their own version of the middle finger; Jack could be flipping him off and he wouldn't be the wiser. Then again, it doesn't sound like a Jack thing to do, if only because Jack would want him to *know* it.

It takes a few seconds before Jack settles, and then he's back to the face that George has grown familiar with over the past few weeks. Strong jaw, tawny skin, dark eyes—all of it leaves George feeling warm with glee.

Jack crosses his arms and sighs, looking so much like a disappointed parent that it's a little disturbing. "This is the fourth time, George."

"I know, I know, but I actually have a job for you this time!"

Jack quirks an eyebrow. "Yeah? What is it?"

"Well…" George drags out the word, casting his gaze up to the ceiling innocently. "See, I really feel like going out for dinner tonight, right? Only problem is, I'm broke."

"You have a job."

"Yeah, and the cash isn't exactly flowing since they're still trying to find someone to replace Sawyer." If he's being honest, George thinks the new guy they've brought in to fill Sawyer's vacant job seems like a good choice. Henry Markieren is a big man with a good temper and a level head. He'll do well in the position. And George will say as much to anyone who'll ask, but Jack doesn't need to know all the gritty details.

He has to believe George has a somewhat-valid reason for calling him here—unlike the last time George contracted him, where his only terms were that he needed help getting in the shower. (Because he could, mostly, and because the idea of showering with Jack was more than appealing. All of his fantasies involved Jack taking his clothes off for him and hand-feeding him from a bowl of cherries as he washed his hair, but that hadn't even come *close* to happening. Jack had dumped him in the running shower, fully clothed, then proceeded to laugh at him until George came out sulking like a drowned cat. A valuable lesson was learned that day: demons are sneaky bastards.)

"Dammit, George. I keep telling you that you can't keep contracting me like this."

"Yeah, I know that! You don't give me any other way to reach you. It isn't like I can just text you whenever I've got some brilliant joke to share, so I have to do it face-to-face. You don't make things easy, you know."

Jack rolls his eyes and nods to the barrier of the circle. With a smirk, George drags his toe through it. A tension in the air lifts, and Jack strolls out like he's stepped into his second home. Gone is the tension that left him so uncomfortable the first few times George contracted him here. Now he's gotten used to the place, and to George's friendliness.

"I'm so sorry you're running low on ways to bug me."

"Yeah, you should be. I dunno how you can live without me hanging around you."

"I'll manage," Jack drawls, "somehow."

Sighing, George crosses his arms over his chest. "Otherwise I'm just gonna have to keep contracting you. Since you seem to hate that so much...."

"Has it occurred to you," says Jack, "that I just don't like you?"

There's something George knows isn't true. He holds Jack's gaze for a long few seconds before smirking. "Nah."

Jack opens his mouth to retort, but something cuts him off—a distinct hum. Jack's hand flutters to his pocket. It's a quick movement, but George doesn't miss it; he also doesn't miss the eerie electronic glow emanating from inside of Jack's pants, or that this is where the soft buzzing is coming from.

Jack looks sheepish as he draws a familiar object from his pocket. George can hardly believe what he's seeing.

"Wait a second. You have a *phone?*" he demands, blinking incredulously at the device in Jack's hand. The cell phone isn't a brand he's ever seen—it looks very lightweight, with a glowing symbol in neon blue on the back—but it's without a doubt a phone. He isn't sure why he assumed demons didn't have any means of technology; writhing black masses of demonic rage don't exactly preclude modern electronics. Of course, if what Jack says about hell having its own society and culture is true, then it should come as no surprise. Hell, they've probably got their own social media, too. Maybe Jack has a demonic Facebook. Maybe he's verified on Demon Twitter.

Jack freezes with the device in his hand before he looks up at George. "Yeah," he says, slow and hesitant. "What's it matter?"

"Um, holy shit? Jack, gimme your number! This is *so* much easier than doing the circle thing all the time!"

No sooner have the words left his mouth than Jack is drawing back, scrambling to tuck his phone in his pocket. "Nuh-uh. That's not happening."

"Why not?"

"Because you're an annoying ass who's gonna text me stupid shit in the middle of the night while I'm trying to get some sleep."

"Okay, yes," George agrees—while filing away the fact that demons sleep for later—"but I'm also a really good texting buddy."

Jack remains unenthused. "We are not going to be texting buddies."

"Jack. Please."

"No."

"*Jack.*"

"It's not happening."

"Come on. Give me your phone!"

Quick as flicking on a light switch, Jack whips his phone out of his pocket and passes it to George's waiting hands. For the space of a second, his face goes slack. He seems not to even realize what he's done until his hands are empty and George is eagerly typing his number into Jack's contact list.

He shoots himself a quick text and takes a selfie for his contact photo for good measure, before passing it back to Jack. He finds the demon glowering at him. Jack accepts his phone back and tucks it right back into his pocket, like he's afraid George will actually try to steal it.

"Don't do that," Jack snarls, and George blinks in confusion. "That direct order shit. You know I have to obey those, and it's not fair."

It takes George a moment to realize what Jack is talking about. Then he registers the real hurt on the demon's face, and it all floods back to him.

This is another term of the contract he hadn't realized existed until further exploration ensued. While a contract is standing, Jack has to follow whatever direct orders George gives—whether it's something as simple as "sit down" or as complex as "jump out the window." As soon as George discovered this power, he grew disturbed and swore to Jack he would never use it without his consent. George may have a lot of ideas for things he could do with Jack's help, or just *with Jack,* but no way would he ever take advantage of him.

George feels a stab of guilt in his ribs and tries to brush it off before it can cut too deep.

"Shit, man," he mutters. "Sorry. Slipped my mind."

"Yeah," Jack says, giving him a smile carved from stone. "Bet it did."

"Jack," George says, but the demon shakes his head.

"It doesn't matter. I told you already, I don't care."

"No, it does matter. I wouldn't do that to you, ever. Not without your permission." He can see Jack starting to drift away, closing off from him. George has learned enough about Jack by now to know that when his shields go up, there's no easy way of getting them down, and he doesn't want to let him slip away tonight. "That was wrong. I'm sorry, and I won't do it again."

Jack sighs in the face of George's earnest expression. It's not much, but it's enough to restore George's confidence, as well as his enthusiasm.

He holds out an arm, offering it like a gentleman in any classy 1940s movie. He may be no Cary Grant, and Jack is definitely not Katharine Hepburn, but George hopes his inner charm can make up for that. He offers Jack a wink and a small smirk. "What do you say? Will you come out with me tonight?"

Jack hesitates for only a second before his face hardens into a resolved expression. He takes George's arm, and there is a flicker in his eyes that almost looks like amusement, though it only lasts a second.

"Not like I could get rid of you if I tried," Jack mutters, and George's grin grows broad and bright.

"OKAY. EXPLAIN TO me what you do for work again."

It might be the terrible lighting in this restaurant, but George is sure he sees Jack's eye twitch. His job is a definite sore spot for him. He doesn't talk about it often, and when he does, it's never in much detail. George has gathered just enough information to figure out that Jack has a desk job, which is so unsuited to him that it's almost hilarious.

"I told you. I process reports of infiltrations into the human world throughout all nine quadrants of Hell, and I monitor reports coming in from the more hostile quadrants." He shifts, bristling as though uncomfortable. "A lot of paperwork, but it's vital stuff."

George doesn't doubt it, but there's no way around how much deskwork doesn't suit Jack. He doesn't deserve to be writing reports; he should be the one out there investigating, finding himself in the thick of the action.

Maybe it's awful to tease, but as he leans in he can't keep the grin off his face. "So, basically you're a demonic pencil pusher?"

Jack levels a glare at him, irritation prominent. "It's an important job."

"Oh yeah, sure, no doubt. Just not something I'd imagine you doing, ya know? No offense, but you seem like the kind of, 'punch first, file a report on it later' type of guy."

Jack's knuckles are tight around his water glass, but he doesn't look angry. He looks thoughtful, like George is saying things he's thought a hundred times before himself. "You work at a law firm, you know that's how lawsuits happen."

"Can't argue with that. But come on, Jack, what is it you really want to be doing? We've all got something?"

Jack rolls his eyes. He's obviously done with this conversation. George doesn't think he's going to get an answer, doesn't expect one—so he's surprised when Jack speaks up anyways. "All demons are trained to be warriors. The stronger you are, the higher you're able to rise in the hierarchy. The higher you are, the more respected you are. I don't give a shit about fame and glory and all that stuff, I could care less... but I always liked being a warrior. If I had my way, I'd be out there fighting. Right on the front lines with the strongest demons. That's the way it's supposed to be."

George bites off the end of a breadstick, staring at him. "Well, what's stopping you?"

"Nothing to fight for," Jack replies giving a rueful little smile. "Lots of arguments, no war. So yeah... I guess I'm stuck being a 'demonic pencil pusher.' It could be worse."

George shrugs his shoulders in an easy, languid motion. "Just seems a little boring for a demon, is all. You know, when there are places to see, people to possess, worlds to terrorize...."

The man in front of him looks wonderfully fed up. "Does all your knowledge about demons come from shitty Hollywood movies?"

"That's my main frame of reference, yeah." George settles back in his seat, shrugging. He's talked to Jack enough about his home that he knows it's not like that at all—Hell, he's learned, is a dense world all of its own, where demons have their own lives, and a lot of better stuff to do than terrorize human beings. According to Jack, there's a movie theatre in his neighborhood, and one of his friends teaches a yoga class. Still, he can never resist goading his favorite demon, just to see the annoyed look on his face.

Jack knows how to strike back, however, and George knows when he sees his dark eye's flash that the serpent's bite is coming. "And what about you?" Jack demands. "Office life. Gotta be living eight-year-old Georgie's dreams, right?"

"You kidding me? When I was a kid, I wanted to be a cowboy."

Jack snorts. George is hit with the memory of himself running around in a cowboy hat and his father's old boots, firing invisible pistols at the old lady who lived next door's flower garden, and he can't help grinning as well. He was a cute kid. "Then I started watching *Bob the Builder,* and I decided, yup, I definitely want to do *that* with my life." At Jack's blank look, he clarifies, refusing to feel sheepish over it. "You know, fixing stuff. Like... not inventing them but making them better. Maybe it sounds a little lame, but I've always been good at putting broken things back together."

Jack leans back in a deceptively casual motion, reclining against the back of the booth. He tucks one arm behind his head, and George fights not to fixate on his biceps. Then Jack takes another sip of water, and George has to struggle not to stare at his mouth instead. He just can't win tonight. "And you wound up doing law firm grunt work instead?"

"Hey, it's a steady paycheck. Boring as hell, but after college my mom was all like"—He pitches his voice up in an impressively awful imitation of his mother's accented motor-mouth—*"Ay, Georgie, tienes que encontrar un buen trabajo!"* which basically translates to, *'you're the oldest, so get a good job and be a role model to your siblings or I'll strangle you till you wish I never gave birth to you.'* Story of my life, right?"

Jack snorts again, to himself this time. "I know that feeling."

Jack never talks about his family, and George doesn't want to push. He doesn't know if demons have families in the same way humans do, since Jack's given him no indication one way or the other. All he knows is that Jack says he lives alone and isn't close to many people. Among the numerous questions George has about Jack, he often wonders if the demon is ever lonely.

"Hey," he says, offering a wry grin. "It's not all bad. You could argue that if it weren't for our shitty jobs, we might never have met."

"Yeah, wouldn't that have been a tragedy."

"Aww, you'd miss me! Come on, you know you would!"

Jack offers him a look that is half tired, half amused. "Maybe I would," he remarks, and George stops cold. His heart, which had been beating a steady rhythm all throughout dinner, suddenly accelerates to a deafening staccato.

Jack gives him a cool smile, and George wonders if his demon isn't a little sadistic after all.

"I knew it," he laughs instead of giving Jack the satisfaction. "You're a big softie. I grow on you, don't I?"

"Like a fungus."

"I'll take what I can get."

That night, their contract ends the same way as every one that has come before it. George asks Jack, *"so what now?"* and Jack replies that it doesn't matter before melting back into the shadows again. George tells himself there's no reason to be disappointed—but he still is, every time.

MAYBE HE IS imagining things, but George often finds himself wondering if his apartment is getting darker.

On some days, he's able to convince himself it's his mind playing tricks on him. On others—the days when shadows stretch long across the halls and floors, consuming everything in their path like the bottomless maw of an insatiable ghoul—the problem is impossible to ignore. He can't write it off as anything else when it's all but evening in his apartment, even as the sun shines high in the sky.

George does not fear the shadows; rather, he is puzzled by them. They were not here a month ago; they were not here a week ago. Day by day, the darkness in his apartment seems to grow denser, and with it comes an oppressiveness that George can't ignore. When the shadows creep nearer to him, he edges away. He replaces all the lightbulbs in his house and tries to ignore how quickly they dim to give birth to new spindly shadows. Sometimes he glances out of the corner of his eye and swears he can see them *move*.

That's ridiculous, he tells himself. Shadows can't move. They can't materialize on their own. Shadows are not living things, capable of consciously following him throughout the house. Shadows definitely can't *hurt* him, no matter what his paranoid brain hisses in the middle of the night.

There's a simple explanation. The building's wiring must be faulty. Isn't that what it always is? Something about the building, or the contractor, or the way his electricity is set up. George resolves to go talk to his landlady at the nearest opportunity to voice his concerns. Maybe someone will actually take care of it.

Which still doesn't explain the nightmares.

He doesn't remember what they're about, not really. They haunt him in flashes. A cloud, inky and oppressive, bearing down on him; black claws dragging over bare skin, leaving gashes that bubble with crimson; bones popping and snapping as they twist at inhuman angles. George hears screams he's sure are his own, sees snapshots of his friends and family dying in a thousand creative ways. By the time he finally pulls himself out of it, waking up is a mercy.

The phantoms of his dreams plague him in daylight hours—every night, however, they seem to get a bit more real. George wakes up in a cold sweat, heart pounding and throat constricted with terror. He has to fight his own body to remember how to breathe. By the time he finally gets control over himself, there's no way he's getting back to sleep—he couldn't if he tried, and he doesn't want to.

So, needless to say, he hasn't been getting much rest the past few nights.

It's taking its toll on him, no doubt. A few of his coworkers have been casting him concerned looks; his mother mentioned that he sounded tired on the phone. George has been jumpier lately, on edge, and he wonders if some of his recent paranoia could be blamed on his lack of sleep.

Or maybe the nightmares and the growing unease are all part of something *else*—something bigger, incomprehensible, uncontrollable. Something terrifying.

George pushes these thoughts out of his head and forces himself to cling to rationality. Faulty wiring. Exhaustion. Maybe he's been eating too much weird stuff before bed. Either way, it's nothing to panic about—whatever is going on will solve itself in time.

Until then, he's going to have to live with what he's got. It's not such an awful deal. He can sleep during the daytime when he can't at night, and the darkness makes that easy. The occasional strains of hissing whispers that float past his ears whenever he's in the middle of a busy task make the apartment feel a little less lonely. The way Dora the cat acts skittish, hissing at empty corners and hiding under furniture, isn't cause for too much concern.

Nothing is wrong, George tells himself. *Everything is just fine.*

And if it wasn't for the tight rubber band wrapped around his chest, getting tighter and tighter every day, he might even be able to believe it.

Chapter Four

THE AIR HANGS heavy over the confined space of the office. It feels thick, charged with tension; as if an invisible coil has wrapped its way around the room, sparking electricity like a fountain spews water. It is not only hard to speak. Formulating thoughts into words is all but impossible, yet even breathing feels like a daunting task in the midst of such oppressive tension.

Winifred Hall has been landlady of Weavenhill Apartments for twenty-three years, coming up on twenty-four this June. She is esteemed among her tenants and trusted by her community. She makes a point to donate to five different charities at the end of each year (among them, a charity for abused animals, one for a children's hospital, and one devoted to helping victims of domestic violence). She sometimes takes a moment out of her day to stop at the store and buy a few cans of food for the handful of stray cats that live behind the building. Her name is well-known among the citizens of the town she's lived in all her life—at least, by those who bother learning local figures' names. Ms. Hall, in the six decades of her life, has been a schoolteacher, a journalist, a writer, and ultimately a landlady. Now she's also a widow, with two children living out of state, and a gaggle of grandkids. She's got a picture of two of them hanging on the wall of her office; there's a little girl in pigtails and a boy with a gap in his teeth, smiling from Grandma's lap.

By all accounts, Ms. Hall is an upstanding citizen. She's a good woman. A kind one.

Lucy Dorsett knows for a fact that Ms. Hall would never hurt anyone.

She also knows that the woman sitting across from her now is *not* Ms. Hall.

She's pretty sure the kindly old landlady wouldn't have a grip like an iron vice, for one thing. She wouldn't have fingernails so razor-sharp that they can dig into the back of her desk chair and come out the other side, as easily as spearing a grape with a toothpick. The veins running along the sides of her face are blue, not black, and she's certain Ms. Hall's eyes shouldn't look like *that*.

The woman trembles with suppressed, furious energy. Her pitch-black eyes glower at Lucy as if she has never seen a more offensive creature in her life and is busy thinking of a thousand and one ways to get rid of her.

Lucy sighs, pushing herself upright in her chair. She does hate it when civil conversations turn ugly.

"I'm sorry," she says to the woman. "I see this conversation has gotten out of hand."

Ms. Hall doesn't reply. Instead, she lunges for her. In one fluid movement, Lucy rolls out of the desk chair and onto the floor, before finding her feet with the smallest amount of effort. Her heels would make a lesser woman stumble, but she's had enough practice that she could run marathons in these girls and not even wobble. She regains her footing and immediately reaches behind her, snagging an iron fire poker from its place against the brick fireplace.

"I'm sorry, Ms. Hall, but I'm afraid we'll have to cut our meeting short."

Face twisted in an impossible grimace, Ms. Hall leaps for her again. Lucy pirouettes back and brings the poker up, slamming it into the old woman's chest. It's not hard enough to gouge, but it knocks the wind out of her. Ms. Hall goes sprawling back, eyes wide and mouth open in a silent gasp. For a second, Lucy is sure she catches a flicker of humanity in her eyes, but it is gone as quickly as it appears.

Of course. Exorcising a demon is never as easy as a little bit of iron and a lot of luck. (A good thing, probably, or else Lucy would be out of a job.)

She draws back for a final blow, but the demon inside Ms. Hall recovers more quickly than she anticipated. Without warning, the possessed woman feels back around and seizes Lucy by the shoulders. She is slammed into the desk headfirst and draws back seeing stars. When she opens her eyes, she is met with unbridled malice turning the woman's face gruesome.

Lucy sniffs and tastes iron in the back of her throat. Her throbbing face hardens into a glare.

Low blows, unfair punches, and demons using their powers to their advantage; those are all things she can tolerate in a fight. There is only one thing she *cannot* abide by. Her blood belongs to her alone; no demon gets to take that from her, no matter what.

Now she isn't just annoyed. Lucy is royally pissed off.

"All right," she hisses and draws back just as Ms. Hall's fist swings towards her face. A well-timed twist is the only thing that keeps Lucy from getting her nose smashed in. As soon as she's out of the most vulnerable position, years of training kick in. Lucy writhes in her attacker's grip, lashes out, as she jabs her elbow hard into her stomach.

No sooner has Ms. Hall reeled backward than Lucy's foot slams into her ribs. The wind is knocked out of her. She stumbles back and almost goes sprawling. When she takes a staggering lunge back towards Lucy, she manages to get her arms wrapped around her neck once more, but Lucy shifts her diminutive weight as she flips her attacker over her shoulder.

Once Ms. Hall is on the floor, it's all child's play from there. Lucy pins her down and sketches an immobilization rune on her forehead with the pen that had been resting on the landlady's desk minutes prior. A bit of holy water is sprinkled, an exorcism rite is read out, and the demon inhabiting Ms. Hall's body escapes her mouth in a rush of dense black smog. It dissipates into the air with a screech and a crackle. Nothing but the low buzz of static electricity is left in its wake.

Lucy pulls herself to her feet, smooths her pencil skirt, and smiles down at the unconscious landlady's body.

Another job well done, if she does say so herself.

She breezes out of the landlady's office with unflinching ease and does not look back as she shuts the door behind her. Her heels clack against marble floors, tracking her path through the lobby. She takes a moment to pause in front of a mirror mounted on the wall, straightening out her suit jacket and adjusting her blonde curls, before continuing down the hallway.

The apartment building is not large, or well-decorated, or cheap. There is nothing unusual about its design, its furniture, or—as of two minutes ago—its management. There is nothing special about this building.

She bypasses the elevator and heads straight for the stairs. There is no doubt that she is headed in the right direction. The pendant around her neck—tucked just out of sight beneath her buttoned blouse, safe against her breast—has been pulsating with energy from the moment she stepped into the building. It is no longer as strong as it was in the landlady's office, but as she ascends the stairs, the pendant grows warmer and warmer.

She stops at the sixth floor, nods to herself, and opens the door. The hallway stretches in front of her, a repetitive sequence of bare walls and wooden doors.

Stand tall, she reminds herself. *Shoulders back, eyes front. Walk like you belong here, and no one will ever suspect you don't.*

Lucy's mother tells her often that she should have been an actress. She has a point. From a young age, Lucy always took to the stage with energy, enthusiasm, and—most importantly—skill. It was never the spotlight that enthralled her. What really beckoned to Lucy Dorsett from the moment she first learned to play pretend, was the chance to become someone else. Playing another role gives her the chance to shed her skin. For a little while, she can be a completely different person; another life, another name, thoughts and feelings and memories that are not her own. Slipping through different identities like water isn't just a talent. It's an art, and Lucy has it honed to perfection.

There are some roles Lucy loves to play. She loves being *"the soon to be Mrs. Lucy Lee,"* affectionate fiancée of Henry, doted upon and loving in return. She adores being *Lucy Dorsett,* who greets every customer at the bookstore with a smile and warmly gives regular customers permission to use her nickname. For years she thrived in the role of *"our Lou,"* the straight-A student and dedicated daughter. These are the identities that are hard to slip in and out of... because she adores them so much.

It's the inconsequential ones like these that she finds she prefers. Realtor, lawyer, secretary, college student, even prostitute—these are all easy, faceless tasks. Names run together like water, even if her face stays the same. She doesn't get close to any of these people, the aliases and identities she doesn't care to connect with. She doesn't see into their heads, their hearts. She only becomes them for a little while and then slips away to her ordinary life once more. They are other roles she has to play.

No, Lucy would not have made a very good actress after all.

605, she echoes in her head. Sharp green eyes scan the hallway, searching for the number in question. *605. Apartment 6-0—*

A sudden buzz from her phone does not manage to startle her, but it distracts her concentration. Brows furrowed, Lucy pulls the device from her purse. Her frown fades as she recognizes the familiar name on her screen.

Henry, 8:14am: date night tonight! I'll make dinner around 6???

Lucy feels a smile take over her lips. She wouldn't be unable to erase it, even if she tried. Henry never ceases to surprise her with little dates or gestures; even something as simple as making dinner can turn into an adventure with him. Sometimes she wonders if he lives to make her life exciting.

to Henry, 8:15am: wouldn't miss it for the world!!! ;) love you <3

Henry will be waiting for her at the restaurant, probably with a fresh bouquet of flowers (there is a florist's shop across the street from the elementary school, and he often stops there after work). She ought to get this job done early, then. It would be a shame to keep him waiting.

As she tucks the phone back in her pocketbook, her gaze finally finds 605. A tiny hum of satisfaction escapes her.

There is no hesitation before she raps on the door. Her knuckles make a sharp, hollow sound against the wood, and she counts to five in her head before knocking again. If she has to, she'll break out her hairpins and open the door herself, but she'd rather not go that far before she's certain no one is home.

Sure enough, on her second round of knocking, the door opens.

"Hi there," she greets the scruffy-haired man in the doorway. She flashes him a smile, all pearly teeth and warmth, and sees his shoulders relax without his notice. "My name is Hannah Archer, and I'm with the building inspection committee. Can I ask you a couple of questions about your living situation, Mister...."

"Call me George," the man provides. "George Soto."

She's tall enough to see over the man's shoulder. His apartment is dark, but she catches a flash of white marks on hardwood floors just in view of the doorway. She's too far away to make out the sigils, but the sight of a circle is familiar. The pendant around her neck sears against her skin like hot coal, and her smile widens.

"Mister Soto," Lucy amends. "Would it be all right if I came in for a minute?"

Chapter Five

HE WINDS UP twenty minutes late for work.

If Sawyer were still around, he would have caught hell for it. Thankfully their new boss is more laid back. He let him off with a warning, but George is still unhappy about it. He's got a stronger work ethic than that; he should, and can, do better. He shouldn't let himself be distracted by some building employee showing up at his apartment, interrupting his morning routine, and asking a bunch of questions before darting off as soon as she came. Sometimes he can't stand living in an apartment. He hopes Hannah Archer found what she was looking for, whatever that was.

At the end of the day, he's still a bit annoyed with himself for being late. It's no skin off his back, but he's going to make a better impression tomorrow.

George makes his way down the back stairwell on the way out of work. He hates the back exits; they are narrow and winding, lit by fluorescent lights which serve to make the stairwell no less unnerving. It's a quick way out, however, and he feels like leaving work quickly. As he's pushing the heavy metal door which leads into a back alley open, his phone chimes.

George pulls his phone out of his pocket, casting a quizzical frown at it. There are a few texts from his friends, one from his sister, two garbled ones from his mom—and one from Jack.

It's nothing more than a response to what George sent him earlier, but the sight of Jack's message makes him smile. It means Jack is taking the time out of his day to talk to him when he doesn't have to. Jack bothers to answer. He *cares* about George—and that really shouldn't make him as happy as it does. George needs to remember how to make friends.

Even Jack's blunt reply of, *"quit texting me, don't you have work??"* is better than nothing.

George can't help smiling as he tucks his phone into his pocket. He has the feeling that tonight will be a good night. Maybe he'll go out—he doesn't like spending time alone in his apartment nowadays, but there's always something to do. The local fair is in town. He can have some fun there, if he can rope one of his friends into going with him....

The shadows are the first thing he notices. Sure, he's been feeling surrounded by mysterious shadows everywhere for the past few weeks, but this is different. These come without the oppressive sensation of the air being smothered out of his lungs; the alley does not grow darker, like night descending in the space of a single breath. Instead, the light is simply... blocked out.

He looks up to see three hulking men standing at the mouth of the alley.

George's stomach drops. They're staring at him, there's no question about that, and they're looking for a fight. George grew up the scrawny kid in a rough neighborhood, so he knows how to recognize when a group of guys are dying to hit something. Right now, he's the only target in sight. They're locked on him.

Dammit, he thinks, *who the hell picks a fight with a guy carrying a briefcase?*

He knows how to throw a good punch, but the odds here are not in his favor. It's three against one, and the smallest of these guys is still as big as two of him.

Behind him, the locked back door of his office building. Ahead of him... well, nothing nice. A grimace settles over George's face as his situation dawns on him.

There's exactly one way out of this situation. He doesn't like it, but he's got no other options.

He has to play dumb.

So instead of turning on his heel and running, like any reasonable human with a pulse and healthy will to live would, he marches up the alley, right towards the group of men. He even puts a spring in his step as he goes, swinging his briefcase at his side. When he reaches them, he grins.

"Hi, guys! Nice night out here, isn't it?"

He was hoping to throw them off, and it worked—to a point. One man looks confused, but the other two remain focused. When their glares lock on him, George feels like an antelope in the sights of a lion pride. They take a step together, blocking his sight of the street. A heavy feeling settles in the pit of George's stomach.

"Gimme your wallet," says the biggest of the guys. George is a little disappointed at his lack of creativity.

"Yeah, see, I'd really like to, but—"

"Give up your wallet now, or we blow your head off! You hear me?"

By the startled look one of the thugs shoots the speaker, George feels safe to guess that no one here actually has a gun. Not safe enough to call their bluff, however; he's stubborn, not stupid. "Come on guys, all I've got is a few dollars and a Taco Bell coupon—"

"Wallet. *Now!*" bellows the largest one, starting towards him, and George takes a wide step back, holding up his hands.

"Okay. Fine, you got it." Slowly, he reaches into his pockets. The last thing he wants is to be proved wrong about the gun, though he's pretty sure the big one could take his head off with one punch. (Dammit, he really needs to go to the gym more.) "Here it is. Here."

He extracts the wallet from his pocket slowly, letting the thugs see it. The alley is getting darker, so he has to flash the front cover up into the sparse light. They don't notice.

"What else you got on you?" one of the guys demands. George's eyes are locked on the space over his head.

"Just my shining personality," he replies.

"You think this is a game?"

"Could be. I dunno." He shrugs, taking another step back. "You feel like playing?"

"Son of a—" starts the big one, and lunges—either to take George's wallet or plant a fist in his face—but he freezes when another hand locks around his wrist.

The most alarming part might not be the color of the hand—an inky pitch black that seems to waver like smoke when you stare at it—but the fact that blade-like claws twine up his wrist, leaving gashes in the sensitive skin. The thug gapes for a moment, unable to move, unable to breathe. Slowly, he turns around.

"This is why humans are fuckin' ridiculous," Jack says, and punches the guy right in the face.

George was expecting something a little more demonic—maybe a few explosions, blood pouring from various openings, a bit of *excitement*. This works too.

"The next time you—" Jack says and swings a fist into the next guy's eye— "call on me for something—" The big one still hasn't gone down and catches Jack's knee in his stomach— "this damn *stupid*—" Jack slams the guy's head into a wall, problem solved— "I'm just not gonna come."

The one who tries to run gets knocked out by an entire trash can flying across the alley towards him—*there's* the excitement George has been waiting for. Static screeches in his ears as the three battered, unconscious crooks are levitated off the ground. Jack seems to debate for a few seconds before depositing them neatly on the roof of George's ten-story office building.

"Umm, there's no way to get down from the roof," he points out, somewhat belatedly.

Jack smirks. "Good."

Slipping his wallet back into his pocket, George can't keep the grin off his face. No matter how many times he sees Jack in action, he never gets any less cool. Jack could crush him like a bug, and George is *so* okay with that. When he turns to his savior, Jack looks less than amused, but this is his default state. George isn't worried.

"You know how I summoned you to 'cash in on a favor later'?" he asks.

"This was that favor."

George claps his hands. "Nope! Not quite, but way to go anyway. I knew I could count on you."

Jack grits his teeth. "What," he says, "is the favor, then?"

By now, he's so used to Jack's... Jack-ness that he's not put off a bit. Being prickly, antisocial, and awkward is Jack's *thing*. George's thing is dragging him out of his shell and getting him to experience the joys of humanity a little. So far he's been met with startling success, even if he still hasn't figured out how to get Jack into the shower with him. (All great ambitions take time.)

He seizes hold of Jack's arm but rethinks it when he's met with a raised eyebrow. "I wanna take you somewhere," he says anyways, even if Jack looks less receptive about the idea.

True to form, Jack reacts in his quintessentially Jack manner. George wouldn't expect anything less. "I'm not going anywhere with you," he retorts, turning on his heel. "I did my job. Now I'm going home."

"That? That was your job?"

"Protecting you is my job, yes."

"All you did was punch a few guys! Like that's anything for you!"

Jack casually slips his hands into the pockets of his jeans. "Next time I'll let you get your face smashed in. My mistake."

George mutters something frustrated and not very intelligible under his breath—a side effect of growing up in a household where Spanish is spoken more than English. (He knows a lot of old Colombian curses that would make his mother slap him and his *abuelita* proud.) His feet pound against the pavement after Jack, chest heaving with the exertion. Not only is Jack tall and muscular, but his lean legs are also built for distance. In George's (short) personal opinion, this makes him twice as annoying.

When he finally catches up, Jack is already out of the alley and strolling along the sidewalk, hands still tucked into his pockets. He barely glances over his shoulder as George falls into step next to him.

"Come on. Are you really... leaving?"

"What do you want me to stay for?" Jack asks, but he doesn't sound as annoyed anymore. Maybe George's persistence is paying off. There's a note of genuine curiosity in Jack's voice that he can't hide, and it's the opening George needs. He seizes upon it.

"The fair's tonight, you know. The Summer Bonanza, the same one the town puts on every year. It's got rides and games and prizes, a pretty basic thing, but it's a blast—"

"What's a fair?" Jack interjects. George stops cold, jerking his companion to a halt with him.

"You're kidding." He has to choke on the words to get them out; from the way he gapes at Jack, any curious stranger would think he just mentioned growing a second head. Jack's expression betrays no humor; the genuine confusion on his face is impossible to fake. "You're not kidding," George concludes, shaking his head. "Well, now there's definitely no choice."

"No choice in what?" Jack takes a wary step back, but George's grip around his forearm won't let him go far. Jack blinks in the face of it, looking baffled.

Maybe George doesn't have much of a social life nowadays, but he still remembers how it's done. Hell, showing his dates a good time is woven into his DNA. If Jack has really never been to a fair before, and this is his first time, he needs to have the experience of a lifetime. No one is better suited for this monumental task than George Soto.

A slow, wicked grin spreads across George's face. Jack blinks down at it like a deer in the headlights of an oncoming car. As George's hand tightens around Jack's bicep, he cackles.

"Oh, we are going to have *fun*."

THROUGH RELENTLESS INTERROGATION, George has figured out that demons don't have all that many weaknesses. They're not bothered by fire; praying gives them a headache; holy water just makes them mad, but George figures *he'd* be pretty pissed off too if someone splashed water in his face while screaming at him. Jack also can't be killed by the normal fun stuff, like guns or knives, or even a stake to the heart.

(*"That's a vampire thing. That kills vampires."*
"No, I'm pretty sure it's an everyone thing."
"It specifically kills vampires."
"A branch through my heart would specifically kill me,
too. Just saying.")

In other words, there's very little that can actually do harm to Jack. Thanks to this, he isn't afraid of much. When George showed him some horror movies, he laughed so loud that George worried the neighbors were going to complain. (He won't deny that hearing Jack laugh was like watching puppies bouncing on a trampoline. It made him feel warm and thrilled and happy all at the same time, like he accomplished something very few people get to claim. If that's all it takes to make Jack happy, he'll gladly stay up all night watching clips of horror movie classics.)

Jack does have a weakness though. Everyone does. George knew his weakness was out there—he just didn't know when he'd find it, or how.

He may have just figured it out.

"Okay," says Jack, doing an about-face and beginning to walk in the opposite direction. "Let's *not* go here. Let's get the hell out of here."

George's tight grip on his arm jerks him backward. When Jack rounds on him, he lets his eyes flash black, just for a second.

George cuffs him on the head anyway. "Whoa, hey! What's the matter with you? You wanna go shouting, 'hey, look at me guys, I'm a demonic hellbeast' from the rooftops? We're in public. Keep the eyes away." When Jack opens his mouth to protest, he cuts him off with a stern, "Nope. Away."

(And George's mother said he never learned anything from her....)

Instead of going Full Demon again, Jack just squares his shoulders and glares at him. It ought to be more intimidating than it is. George isn't sure if he's gotten used to Jack at this point or is just so certain he wouldn't hurt him, but his glare has little-to-no effect on him. He frowns back, raising an eyebrow in a clear "what's your problem?" gesture.

"I," says Jack, "am not going near that thing."

"What thing?" says George.

"That," Jack enunciates, and points.

He's pointing, George realizes after a few seconds of disbelief, at the dragon coaster. Everybody in town knows the dragon coaster. It's one of the less extreme rides that comes to the fair every year, just enough of a thrill for little kids to shriek on it, while not being too boring for preteens. By the time kids enter their teenage years, they've mostly grown out of the thrill of hunching in tiny painted cars and listening to the dragon roar as he drags himself over rickety tracks, vanishing into a tunnel before coming out the other side. It's a fun ride, but it's definitely not scary, or all that exciting.

Yet for some reason, Jack looks absolutely terrified of it.

Like, quaking in his boots. Ready to run off screaming. About to swoon like a Victorian lady who's just learned her husband has been run over by a horse-drawn carriage. Jack looks *scared out of his mind.*

George isn't a nice person. The laugh that bursts from his mouth wouldn't be out of place coming from a hyena. "The kiddie dragon coaster," he clarifies. "You're *afraid* of the kiddie dragon coaster? Jack. Buddy. Six-year-olds go on that thing. You are a grown-ass demon, and you're scared of the kiddie dragon coaster?"

"*Yes*," Jack fires back, and takes a big enough step back that George winds up getting dragged along with him. Once he realizes he is not being anchored by George, and can actually move him, Jack starts retreating at a pace that would make the French army proud. George gets dragged for all of ten steps before he digs his heels in. When that fails to work, he slams his heel directly onto Jack's toes.

Poor Jack lets out a yell loud enough to draw the attention of a cluster of kids away from their cotton candy. George feels no sympathy for him. His hands lock around tense shoulders as he forces Jack to look him in the eyes.

"Jack," he says, slow and careful, like he's negotiating with a spooked horse instead of a reasonable adult. "You're here with me, okay? We came out to have fun. I'm not gonna let a dumb roller coaster ruin our fun, but I'm also not about to let my big strong demon date be scared of it. Look at me, hey." He taps Jack's cheek when he tries to turn his head. Jack's eyes widen in disbelief, but he's looking at George again. George forces as much seriousness into his voice as possible. "I promise," he declares, "that I will not let the scary dragon hurt you."

Jack's stares back at him, flat and expressionless. George has to fight the urge to giggle again.

"I promise, okay?" He holds out his hand. Jack stares at it like he's spent an hour petting plague rats.

"I don't trust you," he says after a moment. George accepts this benevolently.

"I know. That's smart. So, you coming with me, or am I riding Puff the Magic Dragon all by myself?"

Jack—like George knew he would, because when it comes down to it, he thinks he really does know Jack—sighs and takes his hand. As George leads him to the ride, he's a little too gleeful.

Hearing Jack shriek along with a dozen preschoolers as the tiny coaster makes its way over the three-foot drop makes it all worth it. George can't keep the grin off his face for the entire ride; especially because Jack's vice grip on his hand doesn't loosen up once.

GEORGE IS AS terrible at carnival games as he's ever been. That doesn't stop him from blowing half his wallet on the pursuit of coveted cheap stuffed animals. He insists it's the principle of the thing; you play games to win, and you don't stop until you win something, damn it. He also insists that the games are all rigged, and he'll stand by this statement on his deathbed.

He tears through the ring toss, the dart throw, the water gun game. Even that game with the basketballs (and George is good at basketball) leaves him empty-handed. More of his cash vanishes into the booth supervisor's hands, and he tries and fails until shame sends him to the next stall.

At one point, one of the balls bounces back and hits him in the face. He almost breaks his glasses and is going to have a nice bruise tomorrow. They leave that stall *real* quick.

"This is the most pathetic thing I've seen in my life," declares Jack after George fails to knock over the tower of milk bottles, yet again. As the baseball bounces off the backboard and hits the floor, George grimaces. When Jack sighs, he turns his displeasure on him.

"Why don't you try it, tough guy, huh? It's all rigged. I swear to God, it's a scam. All of it."

"It'd help if you actually hit the balls," says Jack. George sends him a withering glare.

Nonetheless, he passes over his last baseball. Jack weighs it in his hand, frowning as he studies the scuffed exterior.

"I told you," George mutters. "The balls are weighted. You can't throw 'em right, they won't hit anything."

Jack looks thoughtful. "That's what they do, huh?"

He takes a step back, returning his gaze to the bottles. His eyes narrow; his shoulders square. The muscles in his arm flex as he winds up, and George isn't going to lie—it's really attractive.

At least, it would be, if it weren't for the spark of lightning he spots flashing across Jack's dark eyes right before he throws.

The ball hits the tower dead center. Bullseye. The bottles go crashing to the ground, making a terrible racket as they fall. Jack swipes his hands together, smug.

"Very difficult," he says, flashing George a wink.

He cheated, and George knows it. They both know it—but does it really matter? The game was conning them anyway, so why shouldn't Jack scam them right back? (Having a demon around, George can't help but think, comes with more perks than Jack's pretty face and exquisite social graces.)

Besides, now they get to pick out a prize. George has been dying to win something all night, and the array of T-shirts spread before him could not look more tantalizing.

"This is the best thing I've ever seen," he announces, holding an Iron Man shirt up to Jack's shoulders. His chest is about as wide straight through as it is across; the shirt will barely fit and will cover nothing. It's perfect, George decides.

Jack doesn't look as thrilled with his new prize as George is. Understandably, he looks confused. "What is this?"

"It's a T-shirt, genius. You're wearing one right now." George plucks at the collar of Jack's casual black T-shirt before scrutinizing the shirt in his hands. "Huh. Do you think you'd look better in another one? I think you could rock the Minions shirt—ooh!" A small, light-colored shirt emblazoned with the face of a grinning snowman snatches George's attention immediately. "This is perfect. Who doesn't love Frozen, right?"

Jack blinks at him. It takes George longer than it should to realize he's got no idea what he's talking about.

His first reaction is undiluted astonishment. Then he finds himself grinning, and the expression on Jack's face shifts to one of (appropriate) alarm.

"We are having a movie marathon. Next time I see you it's gonna be popcorn, butter, and the entirety of my DVD collection. It's happening. Be ready."

Twisting out of George's reach, Jack holds up the Frozen T-shirt. "Are we getting this or not?"

George takes a moment to consider the idea of Jack actually wearing *that*.

"Yes," he says. "Oh yeah, we are *so* getting it."

ONCE THEY'RE DONE with the games, they tear through the fair without mercy or regret.

Jack is the best possible person George could have invited, because ninety percent of the time he has no clue what's going on. The dunk tank baffles him ("So, you humans toss balls in a game to try and drown each other? That's sick."); the bumper cars thrill him, though he doesn't quite get the point ("Everyone else is in cars! How are you supposed to run people over?"); and he's both amused and disgusted by cotton candy. ("This stuff is the most disgusting thing I've ever eaten. This isn't food," he declares while shoving more cotton candy into his mouth.) George gets to show him around, pointing out his favorite attractions while steering him away from the worst ones ("Not the swings. We don't trust the swings.")

It's *awesome*.

George's favorite dates have always been ones where he can relax and not have to make a fantastic impression on anyone. Being with Jack... is like that. It comes with no pressure because the demon doesn't care enough about human social graces to really care how George acts around him. Jack will roll his eyes when George tells a bad joke or when he trips coming off the hang gliders; he'll yell when George leans too far forward on the Ferris wheel (a delightfully human reaction), but George does not spend the night feeling like he has to impress anyone. There's no reason to put on a show. There is simply *Jack*.

(And this is a great thing because George has already figured out he enjoys spending time with Jack more than he can say.)

"Where are we going next?" Jack demands, three hours and ten rides later. "Don't you ever get tired?"

"I am fueled by sugar and adrenaline," George retorts, "so I'm pretty much immortal."

"Right," Jack says flatly.

"Besides, you really wanna leave without checking out the best ride in this park?"

"We already went on most of the rides here."

"Yeah, but we haven't gone on *the* ride." The ride that George has been drawn to since he was old enough to come to carnivals in the first place; the one that's always thrilled him like no other.

Jack blinks at the swirling blur of colors and lights doubtfully. "*The Cra-Zee Spin?* What the hell is that?"

George says nothing. He allows Jack to watch as the circular ride decreases in speed, slowly returning to the level earth until it's back on the ground once more. The disoriented riders stumble off, some looking queasy, others on the verge of giggling hysterics.

"Huh," says Jack. "Back home, we call that a torture device."

"Hell's gotta be one big carnival, then," George retorts, dragging Jack along by his hand. "C'mon, buddy."

Jack takes his sweet time following, but George understands his hesitance. The ride looks terrifying from the outside; he remembers how his child self always stared up at it with a mix of awe and horror. That was before he was old enough to ride, and realized how *fun* it is. *The Cra-Zee Spin* is his favorite ride bar none, and twenty-six years of carnivals have never let him down. Jack is going to love it.

"You fasten this here," he shows, helping Jack adjust the safety strap across his waist. "Then you just stand against the wall. You don't have to hold on or anything, just... wait for it. And don't be weird, huh? Don't, like... get scared and make something explode. Again."

"I wasn't expecting the clown to pop out," Jack grumbles. George tries not to think of how the Haunted House of Mirrors is now missing about twenty shattered mirrors, and focuses on the ride at hand.

"Just don't get scared. I promise this is gonna be great."

Nothing about George's promises have a history of working out well for Jack. Not even a little bit. Jack knows this, because he shoots George a wary look out of the corner of his eye. George winks back at him.

There is a slight jerk as the ride starts up. Jack's hands tighten suddenly on his safety belt, eyes widening. George can't help the grin that spreads across his face.

"Don't have a heart attack!" he calls out—and that's all he gets the chance to say before the ride begins to spin.

It's exhilarating. An utter rush. Euphoria. There is no better way to describe the way George's heart seems to leap in his chest, the way his stomach swoops and his body floods with adrenaline. Gravity pushes him back against the wall, and he lets out a laugh as air moves past him in a great rush. Lights begin to flash. The world outside the ride turns into one great blur the faster the contraption spins.

He twists his head to look over at Jack and finds him wide-eyed, face ashen, gripping the belt for dear life. The ride is beginning to tilt. Jack squeezes his eyes shut, and George cannot hold back a peal of laughter.

Every part of him feels electric. He can hear the shrieks of his fellow riders, but that is nothing compared to the sound of his heart pounding in his chest. It is a frantic drumbeat, drowning everything else out. The rest of the world spins on, and George is not confined to his body, to the rush of blood and hammer of pulse, but something greater. It feels like he's flying.

And then the floor drops away.

He was prepared for this, too—but as the bottom of the ride vanishes and he can suddenly see the ground far below him, something seems to slip out of place. He cannot pinpoint the moment his exhilaration turns into real terror. Maybe it's the shock that does it—going from solid ground below him to not in the blink of an eye. He knows it's an illusion, he *knows*, but panic still seizes him in a vice anyway. It is as if someone has wrapped their hand around his throat and squeezed.

He looks up, and that's when the fear becomes real.

He is alone on the ride. The dozens of other riders from seconds before have vanished. Their screams still echo in his ears, but the rest of the ride is empty; no one else is pressed to the wall, laughing or holding on for dear life. Even Jack, seconds before a solid presence at his side, is gone. An undone safety belt dangles in the place he should be.

George's eyes widen; the smile slips off his face. Suddenly his lungs feel as if they've inhaled a cloud of winter air. His throat is thick with ice, and his heart, his heart...

He squeezes his eyes shut. When he opens them again, Jack is at his side, shell-shocked expression set on his face.

"George!" he hollers over the shrieks of the other riders. "I don't like this!"

His voice is almost lost in the roar of wind, but it is still the sweetest sound George has ever heard. He turns his head and is met with the other riders, just as they should be. His heart is still in his throat.

"I —" he tries. His voice dies. Jack could not hear him anyway, and he has no words to describe what he just saw. He takes a deep breath and tries to ground himself in reality. The stars are glittering overhead. He looks up.

A jolt hits him, like an ice-cold hand plunging through his chest, and he's back again- Back to the ghostly screams, the deserted ride, and the terror—the numbing, deafening certainty that he is all alone.

Alone, except for something else. Something terrible.

The rainbow of flashing lights illuminate the shadows stretching in each hollow space which ought to hold another rider. The shadows are not people. They do not hold human forms. They writhe and pulse, like some dancing flame, tendrils reaching out to each other but never quite touching. They are as alive as George, but not human. Nothing about them is mortal, or merciful.

George closes his eyes just as he feels something flock around his wrist, and he knows, he *knows* that when he opens them again, he will be back.

Sure enough, Jack is beside him in his next breath. George reaches out, seizing Jack's hand with his own, and tries to root himself in the very real sensation. As long as Jack is beside him, the shadows aren't real. If Jack is here, the ride is not empty, and George isn't alone in the belly of a monster.

Jack's wide eyes turn on him, and confusion flickers across his face. "Are you—"

George blinks, and he is alone. He is holding nothing—but something is holding him. His wrist is ice cold.

He blinks again.

"George?" Jack is closer, face taking up the entirety of George's vision. He looks startled. "What are you d—"

He blinks once more, and it is a mass of shadows churning in front of him. Lightning flashes in front of his eyes; a roar fills his ears, screams and laughter mixed into one. It sounds like someone is being burned alive. Ice is filling him, freezing his blood and embedding itself in his bones.

He blinks again, again, again, but it's still there. It is going to swallow him.

"George!"

Something snaps him back. It is like a rubber band popping back into place. George feels as if he's been shot out of a catapult straight into Jack's arms; he connects with his chest, and Jack has a grip on him in an instant.

The motion of the ride has stopped. The floor is back under George's feet. Above them, the stars have ceased their frantic dance. The other riders are filing off, laughing and stumbling, while the lights have stopped flashing.

The shadows are gone.

"Oh God," George gasps into Jack's chest. He cannot think past the terror, cannot breathe past it. It chokes him. "God, Jack, Jesus, oh God—"

"What is it? What's the matter?"

"I can't!" They're coming for him. He is certain of that. Buried against Jack's chest he can see nothing, but the second he opens his eyes he will be back there, and he will not return. That thing will take him. "I can't, Jack, I've gotta get off—get me off this ride—"

Jack leads him off without asking questions. George stumbles over his own feet, nearly tripping more than once; but he is more focused on choking back sobs, drowning in the solid warmth of Jack's body. He is right there. He is present. He is real, in the same way that the shadow that threatened to consume George was. Jack is solid, and warm, and protects him until they have made it away from the ride, and towards the edge of the fairgrounds entirely.

Only then does George feel able to pull away. He keeps his arms locked around Jack as he opens his eyes. Silhouetted against the night sky, he can make out only shadowy details of Jack's face, but he sees the furrow of dark brows as eyes bore into him. Jack is not just concerned; he's trying to work out what happened for himself.

"I don't know what it was," he pants out. "It was like... I was there one minute, and then the next—and shadows, like something was coming to get me—it wasn't human, Jack, it was—I don't know. I don't know."

"Okay." Jack's voice is hard. His hands, locked around George's shoulders, are grounding. "Okay, George. Time to go home."

George isn't going to argue. He doesn't have the energy; he doesn't know what he could say. After that experience, he's ready to get as far away from the fair as possible.

Jack wraps his arms around him, and George presses himself against his chest again. He doesn't feel them go. It is like the sensation of your plane taking off—a slight swoop of your stomach, the knowledge you were one place and now you are another. It happens in a single exhale. One second, they are at the fair. When George opens his eyes, they are standing in his apartment.

"You're okay," Jack says, steering him towards the couch. "You're gonna be okay."

George sinks onto the couch gratefully and pulls his glasses off his face. He discards them somewhere on the coffee table (he's not paying attention, and honestly doesn't care). The next second, he is pulling himself into a ball.

Jack lingers over him for a moment, not sure what to do. George blinks up at him but turns away after he takes a step back. When he looks up again, the demon has gone.

He isn't aware of much else (aside from Dora wandering into the room, meowing up at him, then jumping on top of the television) for a little while. It is easy to drift in a state of blissful nothing, free of living shadows and parallel dimensions. All he wants to do is hide away, so he does.

Until he feels the press of something soft against his leg, that is.

His first thought is that it must be the cat. It's not the cat.

"Jack," he says slowly, frowning at his legs. "Is that a giant monkey?"

"I went back and got it for you," Jack tells him. He hefts the stuffed animal in his arms (it's almost as big as him), defiantly refusing to be sheepish.

By "*got*," George has the sneaking suspicion Jack means "stole." No matter; he doubts the vendors of the rigged carnival games will miss one giant monkey anyway. He reaches out and locks his arms around it, pulling it to him.

"I love it," he says, burying his face in the downy fuzz.

Jack looks satisfied. He takes a step back, eyes still lingering on George. There is an uncertainty to him, like he is not sure what he is doing here any longer, or if he is really wanted. It obviously isn't a familiar feeling to Jack, but George has seen it before—that first night, when he invited Jack to eat pizza with him.

Now—like then—he does not want to see the demon go.

"Hey, Jack. Wanna do me one more favor?"

"What is it?" Jack asks immediately.

"Stay here tonight."

Jack's brows furrow. George looks up at him, expressionless, exhausted. He wonders if he looks as small as he feels.

After a few seconds, Jack sighs and settles down at the end of the sofa.

Chapter Six

to Jack, 7:38am: heyyyyy babe u up??? ;)
   Jack, 7:39am: george what the fuck
   George smirks down at his phone before setting it on the counter, and looks back up into the mirror. His own reflection gives him a smirk; just the right side of roguish, he thinks, without discrediting the starchy business shirt and tie. He ruffles his hair, doing more to mess it up further than smooth it down, straightens his glasses, and pats the side of a stubble-free cheek. His reflection's smirk widens. Perfect.

He doesn't have to be out of the house until eight o'clock, and work isn't until eight thirty, but he didn't wake up early just to add a little spice of himself to Jack's morning. He's putting an extra effort to make it in on time today. He's still annoyed with himself over being late yesterday, though it was certainly not his fault. Not that he's ever opposed to having a beautiful woman in his apartment—but next time the building inspector visits, he'd rather it be at a time that doesn't throw off his whole schedule. George far from considers himself a creature of habit, but he has making it in to work with just enough time to spare down to an art by now.

Besides, getting up early gives him more time to make sure everything is in order. He looks good; the house looks good; even the cat looks good. He can shower and have breakfast before he has to go in. A normal morning.

Normal. Nobody really appreciates that word, really knows what it means—until suddenly normalcy is a blessing. He couldn't be more grateful for every normal morning. Every second that passes without a flicker of shadows out of the corner of his eye is a gift.

Whatever's been going on lately, he can't worry about it. Whatever *that* was, the night of the fair, all he can do is keep going past it. It hasn't happened again—he hasn't seen anything like that again—so he can only guess it was an outlier. It's not going to happen again, as long as he keeps his head on straight.

As long as everything stays *normal.*

He's out the door before the end of the hour and makes it in to work in half the time it usually takes him. Being one of the first people in the office is strange. The floor seems emptier, somehow, when he isn't greeted by familiar faces first thing in the morning. He settles in to his desk and tries not to shift at the early-morning quiet, but it isn't long before he succumbs to the magnetic pull of the coffee maker.

The small kitchen area, he's relieved to find, isn't as empty as the rest of the office seems to be. The hulking form of Henry Markieren is familiar as he dumps several sugar packets into his coffee and stirs them with a toothpick.

"Hey there, sir," George greets casually; then he notices the beaming grin on his boss's face. "Well, well. Having a good morning?"

"The best, Soto." Markieren turns that wide grin on him. It lights up his face, making him look almost boyish. His grin is infectious; George finds himself smiling back. "Jenny sent me a video right as I got into work. You know I've got a son, right?"

George nods. Markieren will talk at any provocation about his family, specifically his beautiful wife and their infant son. The man starts digging in his pocket, irrepressibly eager, and George smiles as Markieren pulls out his phone. "Look at this. Not even a year old and take a look."

The video shows a baby, round-eyed and bald as an egg, gaping up into the phone screen. At the sound of a woman's voice, he gives a gummy smile and begins babbling a steady stream of incomprehensible noises. The only word George can make out is "banana," and this makes Markieren grin the widest.

"He's wild about bananas, that kid," the man grins. "Just like his old man!"

"Congrats, sir," George says, clapping the man on his shoulder. Markieren returns the gesture with a laugh and goes back to his coffee.

George really does like Henry Markieren. He's not only a competent boss, and a reasonable one, but a good man. In George's opinion, that's what counts the most. The atmosphere in the office has totally changed since Sawyer's abrupt departure, and George is proud to think he had a part in making his coworkers' lives a bit better, however small.

(They still talk about Sawyer's departure in the office. His name is whispered in hushed tones, the story passed around between new interns like some kind of urban myth. Sawyer is quickly fading into legend, and everyone has their own idea of what happened. George employs a rarely-used skill, and keeps his mouth shut.)

George feels revitalized by his conversation with Markieren. As the office fills up again, he finds himself greeting his coworkers with cheer completely inappropriate for this time of the morning. He gets a few glares in reply, and appreciates every halfhearted, "Morning," back.

His day passes by with ease. Morning slips into afternoon with the same familiar monotony George has grown used to since he began working in an office building, and before he knows it most of the office has gone on their lunch break. George—who, in his haste to get out of the apartment today, forgot to grab anything to eat—remains at his desk, working even as the room around him empties out once more.

The floor feels eerie with so few people here. It unsettles him, in a different way from this morning. He can't describe it, but it makes his skin crawl. He feels like he's being watched; he knows it's irrational, but he can't escape the creeping sensation of eyes on the back of his neck.

Restless to do something, he propels himself out of his seat and makes his way down the hallway. The copy room is a small, secluded area at the end of a long corridor, illuminated by large windows that let in the light of day. This afternoon, there's not much sun; the day is overcast, and the lights don't switch on when George walks into the room. He finds himself working in shadow.

It's a nice place to take a break for a few minutes, even if he can't smoke inside the building. He leans against the copy machine and closes his eyes, trying to push the itch out from under his skin. It's stupid to feel uncomfortable, he tells himself. He works here every day. He knows this place, and everyone in it, like the back of his hand. If anyone were watching him—if anyone had a reason to—he would know it.

He opens his eyes again, and maybe it's fate or just luck that lets him catch a glimpse of the woman breezing past the doorway.

The first thing he registers is her face. George has a talent for voices that's unmatched, but he also has a sharp memory for faces. He remembers the little things about people: the curve of their jaw, the dimple in their chin, the freckles on their face.

Hannah Archer—the woman who inspected his apartment building the day before—has a very distinctive shape of her nose: sharp and arched like a ski slope, with a light smattering of freckles across its bridge.

The woman passing him now has the exact same nose. What's more, she has the same honey blonde curls falling to her shoulders, and the same rosy cheeks. She walks in the exact same way: proud, self-possessed, like she's making an effort to fit in with her surroundings and doing it well.

The same woman who was in George's apartment building yesterday is now in his office.

"Hey!" he calls out, pushing away from the printers. "Hang on a minute!"

The woman glances over her shoulder, looks at him, and keeps walking.

You're kidding me, thinks George, staring after the woman in incredulity. Is she actually *running away* from him?

Well, not running—speed-walking, more like, as if she has somewhere important to be and needs to get there right now. George knows better, however; he saw the flicker of alarm in her eyes just before she turned away. She's trying to leave him in the dust.

He does the first thing he can think of, and follows her.

The woman is moving fast, but George is quicker than he looks, with the benefit of not being in high heels. He follows her down the hallway, around corners, and trails her right up to a closed door.

Ladies Room, reads the sign on the door in brassy silver lettering. George stops cold, feeling the wind go out of his sails all at once. If there ever was a roadblock, it's right in front of him.

Slowly, George turns away from the door. There is a part of him that is embarrassed for reacting the way he did. Maybe it wasn't the same woman at all. Maybe he just pursued a random woman through the office for nothing and freaked her out in the process.

No, counters the more reasonable part of his mind. That wasn't the case at all. It's the same woman from yesterday; first she was at his home, and now she's at his office. For some reason, she keeps showing up wherever George is and makes an active effort to avoid him. The question is, why?

This is what George is pondering as he makes his way back to the copy room. The office is still as quiet as before; he makes it two steps into the room before he stops, the realization that the room is no longer empty hitting him like a fist.

It's hard to mistake that powerful frame, even with his back turned to the door. Standing in front of the window, Henry Markieren casts a striking silhouette. "Heya, boss," George greets, grateful for the distraction of another person. "Figured you would have gone to lunch."

Markieren is quiet for a few seconds before speaking. "I didn't feel like it."

"That's fine. No problem." George leans against the printer, casual, until his nose catches onto a familiar acrid smell. He straightens up, eyes scanning Markieren's figure until he catches a glimpse of glowing orange held between his fingers. "Aww, come on. You can steal a smoke break in here, but the rest of us grunts can't?"

"Perks of the job," is all Markieren says. He raises the cigarette to his mouth, and George watches a cloud of foggy smoke billow out to halo his head. Markieren still hasn't turned around; his voice is low, flat, as if he's deep in thought. For a long moment he doesn't speak, and the air seems to grow heavier with each empty second that passes. George frowns at his shoes, suddenly uncomfortable with the silence. It weighs at his clothing, pulling on his hair and sticking to his skin. It's smothering, strangling.

Finally he can't take it any longer. "Hey, you know, I heard this funny joke yesterday—"

There is no warning before Markieren rounds on him. All George sees is a flash of movement, the shadows cast by his boss against the floor turning towards him, and suddenly he has two hundred pounds of Henry Markieren on top of him, pinning him hard against the printer.

"What the—" George starts, but a beefy hand locks around his neck and he *chokes*. Feet scramble for purchase, anything to help him keep his balance, but he finds himself crumbling as Markieren's full weight is pressed down on top of him. The man is almost twice his size and easily doubles his strength. Any attempts by George to claw at the hands on his windpipe are ignored.

Markieren slams him back hard, and a jolt of pain shoots through George's spine. He makes an aborted noise of pain, of fear, but it's cut off when Markieren slams his head against the printer top.

Stars explode in his vision. He can't feel the pain pulsing in his head; the agony of having his throat crushed is far worse, and he's starting to go fuzzy from lack of air. Panic is settling in now. He can't focus on fighting back, on getting away; all he can see is Markieren's face twisted in rage, his *eyes*—

His black, black eyes.

There is no iris, no sclera. Markieren's pupils have expanded to fill up his entire eyes; they are pitch black, ominous shadows churning in their depths. There is no light, no humanity, no trace of the man George knows.

Panic clouds his mind, choking him as effectively as the hand around his neck. This doesn't make sense. Jesus, this doesn't make *sense,* what is happening, *how is this happening—*

His vision is starting to go dark. George fights to stay awake, fights to breathe. If he loses consciousness, he won't wake up again.

In desperation, he kicks out at Markieren's knee. The man barely seems to feel it, but his leg jerks, and this throws him off balance enough for George to slide out from against the printer. He's no sooner on the floor than Markieren is on top of him again, his hands never leaving his neck. George's attacker is forced to double over to pin him on the ground. All George has time to think is that this really isn't a better position to be in; and then a sudden blur flings itself onto Markieren's broad back.

A shriek echoes throughout the room, followed by something connecting with the side of Markieren's temple. The man reacts like an enraged bull; he bucks, hands finally abandoning George's windpipe as he struggles to throw off his assailant. The figure on his back has their arms locked around his neck and they're holding on tight; legs are looped around Markieren's hips, sharp heels digging into his thighs.

Hazy and half-conscious, George follows those legs up to a well-pressed suit, a head of golden curls, and a pretty face twisted in determination.

Recognition has him struggling to sit up, blinking in an effort to regain some coherent thought. The woman on Markieren's back slams his temple again with what George can now see is a paperweight, and Markieren topples over to one side from the blow.

He takes the woman down with him, but she recovers quickly. Using the force of momentum, she straddles his chest and begins fighting to keep him pinned to the ground as the much larger man starts to buck her off.

"Hold still!" she snarls, voice rough from exertion; then, looking over her shoulder, her eyes lock with George. "Help me out!"

George doesn't move. His head is still spinning. He doesn't know what he's seeing.

"Come on! I need your help!"

Jesus, what is happening?

"George!"

It's the sound of his name that snaps George out of his trance. He finds himself lurching forward, reeling on his axis as he moves towards the fight. He helps pin Markieren's shoulders; with the man struggling against him, it takes all of his remaining strength. His hands bear down on Markieren's powerful shoulders, pinning him to the floor, while the woman immobilizes his leg.

George's head is reeling as he watches the woman work. She is brisk, efficient, without a second of hesitation as she whips a clear vial out of her pocket. Water sprinkles over Markieren's head; his struggling suddenly turns to convulsions. George fights the urge to pull away as his boss is caught in the grips of what looks like a seizure, but those wild pitch-black eyes keep him pinned in place. They catch George's own, wide and wild. George finds himself frozen.

It seems like an eternity before the woman sketches a mark across Markieren's forehead in bright red ink. It takes George a second to realize she's using a dry-erase marker, stolen from one of the office desks. She makes a pleased sound at her handiwork, and as quickly as he began convulsions, Markieren goes still once again. There is no hint of struggle, no seizing, and the wildness in his eyes fades. At last, George is able to breathe again.

"Keep holding him," instructs the woman in a crisp, professional tone. Her hands work at Markieren's shirt, undoing the buttons to reveal the broad expanse of his chest, and she quickly begins to sketch out another complicated sigil. "The immobility rune should keep him still, but better safe than sorry."

George tightens his grip on Markieren's shoulders and can only watch as the woman presses her hands on both sides of the sigil across Markieren's chest. In a low tone, she begins to chant—a steady stream of words George can't make heads or tails of, but which flow from her tongue like music.

"*Impius spiritus, exorcizamus te, in nomine Domini et beatus mundi! Et abierunt! Cessa decipere humanas et revertatur ad te mundi diabolica. Hic non receperint vos. Ut mittatur foras, te rogamus, audi nos!*"

With the final word, whatever hold is over Markieren snaps like a rubber band. The blackness evaporates from his closing eyes, fleeing out his mouth in a great burst of foul-smelling shadow. It lingers in the air for a moment, twisting and writhing like something in pain, before it explodes with a fizz and crackle.

George watches the last remnants of ash dissipate in the air, like a firework that died too soon. It leaves behind a smell like rotten eggs that causes his head to spin. Slowly, he pulls himself off of Markieren, who has slumped to the carpet in apparent unconsciousness. He sits on the floor and stares with wide eyes between the crumpled figure of his boss and the panting woman next to him.

"What—" Every breath he takes is ragged. His throat is bruised, windpipe all but crushed; even getting a single word out is a struggle. "What was that?"

"That," says the woman, slapping an exhausted hand on the floor, "was an exorcism."

Exorcism. Like, exorcising demons. George feels faint, and it must show on his face, because when the woman turns to him, there is a flicker in her eyes. It is not sympathy; hell, George doesn't know what it is, but at least her eyes are human.

"What the hell," she says, "do you think you're doing?"

George almost chokes on the breath of air he managed to take. The woman's stare is unfaltering, and he gapes dumbly back at her for a minute before struggling to form a reply. "Who—" he starts, then cuts himself off with a bout of hoarse coughing. The woman waits until he's caught his breath again to answer.

"My name is Lucy Dorsett, and I exorcise demons."

She holds out a brisk hand. He blinks at her; she offers him a nod, obviously expecting him to take it. After a few seconds, George does, and shakes it like he's rattling a delivery box containing a live bomb. Lucy seems appeased, but the grim expression doesn't fade from her face.

"Two days ago I heard a report of demonic activity in an apartment complex downtown, so I went to investigate. It seemed like an ordinary job—some weak earthbound demon that I could send on its way, hardly anything to worry about. I was wrong. What I found was a beehive of demonic energy."

She pauses, frowning at George's face. It's obvious she's gauging George's reaction, but all he can do is blink in bafflement. He's got an idea of what demonic energy is, but that's about it. "Your landlady was possessed, George, did you know that? I had to exorcise her. Then I traced all the demonic energy back to the epicenter, and you know where I wound up? Your apartment."

Now George gives Lucy the reaction she must be looking for. His jaw drops, in shock or confusion, or maybe both. "What?" he rasps, disbelieving. "Me?"

Lucy frowns at him, crossing her arms. He feels like a child once more, being scolded by his mother for something she knows he did. "You know what I'm talking about. I saw the circle on the floor. You've been contracting demons! Don't you realize how much danger you're putting yourself in?"

"Danger?"

George knows that forming contracts with a demon isn't the safest thing in the world, but it hasn't hurt him so far. Besides, he's not contracting random demons to do his bidding for him; he's just summoning Jack. Jack wouldn't do anything to hurt him. He's had more than enough chances, and he hasn't taken advantage of it.

What sort of danger could he be in?

He can't vocalize his thoughts, but his expression makes his confusion clear. Lucy sighs, sitting up a bit straighter. She pats her curls back into order as she talks; George gets the feeling it's more to distract herself than for vanity's sake.

"The barrier between our world and the demonic world is the only thing that keeps what's down there from getting up here," she explains in a matter-of-fact tone. "There are a lot of demons that want to hurt humans—not all, but many. The barrier separating us is crucial, but it's also delicate."

George tilts his head. Lucy waves a hand, fumbling for a useful metaphor. "Think of it like... like a stretched piece of elastic. It's strong, and things bounce off both sides of it without any harm done. But prolonged friction starts to wear away the elastic. Keep working at it, and it gets weaker and weaker, and eventually you get... a hole. A tear. And if there's a tear in the elastic, nasty things can get through."

George blinks; he doesn't know what he would say, even if he could speak. His mind flashes back to his repeated summonings of Jack, all of the warnings Jack had given him not to keep doing it. Jack never said anything about weakening any barriers, and he *never* told George that contracting him could be dangerous!

"I know you're not doing it on purpose—it's obvious you've got no clue what you're doing." (George's nose crinkles, but he's not about to call her wrong.) "Still, you're not just putting yourself in danger, but the entire world!"

It takes a few seconds for the gravity of the exorcist's words to sink in. George settles back on his legs, eyes wide. Lucy is generous, giving him a moment to work through this onslaught of information before she picks up again in that same serious tone.

"As the barrier stands right now, I don't think it's weak enough for anything to get through—aside from a load of demonic energy." She moves towards him, inching around Markieren's unconscious body. Part of George wants to cringe away, but he remains rooted in place. "If you keep this up, I can't say what will happen. It won't be good." Lucy places a firm hand on George's shoulder. "You have to stop summoning demons, George."

His head is reeling. Every word she says only confuses him more, and George wonders if he really hit his head that hard. Maybe Lucy is the one who makes perfect sense, and he's been in the wrong this entire time. Maybe he's unconscious, and these realities of possession and demonic energy are all part of a bad dream.

"What... what will happen?" he asks in a small voice. Lucy sighs.

"Even the tiniest tear in the barrier would be an awful thing." She gestures to Markieren. *"That* would start happening everywhere. If the demons who want to hurt humans get the chance to come through to our world, they will, and they'll cause chaos. Possessions, murder, you name it. It would be a nightmare."

"Why Markieren?"

"Your boss was attacked by an earthbound demon. Same thing with your landlady. Chances are demons are being attracted to you by all the energy you're sweating out. It's clinging to you, like you've been swimming in it. As long as you've got all that demonic energy, you and anyone around you will be targets for stuff like this."

The people around him: his coworkers, his family, his friends. His mind races through a sea of faces, and he feels queasy. "What... do I do?"

"There's only one thing you can do," Lucy replies. "Stop messing around with demons. You can have a normal life, George. All of this can go away."

She sounds sympathetic, which is the worst part. George doesn't deserve her sympathy and doesn't need kindness from her. He finds himself shaking his head before he realizes what he's doing.

"I-I don't know...." He can't stand the idea of putting people in danger, but the idea of never seeing Jack again is a knife twisting in his gut. He can't imagine not being able to talk to him anymore, even if it's just to say good-bye. He isn't sure that would be possible.

"You have to."

Lucy isn't sentimental; he doesn't expect her to be. He's probably not the first idiot she's dealt with. The exorcist presses a card into his hands, and he takes it with numb fingers. "This is my contact information," she says in a kinder voice. "If you need anything, call me, okay? I'm sorry we got off to a rough introduction, but I really am willing to give you any help you need."

"Thanks," George replies, feeling miles away.

A flicker of sympathy crosses Lucy's face again. It makes her green eyes warm, causes that dimple to appear in her cheek, and her brows to crease with worry. She glances her fingertips over his neck, a feather-light gesture, and he hears her sigh. "Go home, George," she tells him. "Put some ice on that neck, get some rest. Stay out of trouble."

The words are familiar, even if the situation is not. He conjures a weak smile—because if there's anything George Soto knows how to do, it's make light of a seriously screwed up situation. "I'll do my best."

Do his best. He's come damn close to breaking the universe and hurting the people closest to him. If this is George's best, he's terrified of what his worst must look like.

Nonetheless, Lucy smiles. She has a face made for smiling; it makes her look younger, flatters her round cheeks and warm eyes. Slowly she pulls herself off the ground and helps him to his feet after her. He's still shaky; he braces himself against the printers as she smooths herself down, brushing off her skirt and straightening her blouse. She makes it look so easy, as if she hasn't just dropped the bombshell of the universe on him.

She seems eager to go, catches herself in the doorway. Manicured nails dig into the frame; her spine is an iron rod of tension. A second of hesitation passes before Lucy turns back again to regard him with kind eyes. Her expression is serious once more, but her voice is soft. "George—be careful. Remember that everything you're doing has a price. You've got to be prepared to face it."

This is what she leaves him with: a quiet warning, a mind reeling with questions, and bruises blooming across his neck.

SHE TAKES THE way out of the building that she knows will keep her from being caught by any security cameras: down the back staircase, which leads out into an alleyway. She walked into the building through the front doors, but with the risk of someone having seen her take down Markieren, she's in no hurry to exit the way she came.

Her heels clack against each step as she descends the winding stairs. She can still taste the adrenaline in her throat; she fights to swallow it back, though the exhilaration of a successful job tastes sweet. She knows she just rattled George Soto's foundations, and her news obviously devastated him. The heartbroken look that flashed across his face at her warnings had been impossible to ignore. It had been a necessary evil, however. When it comes to demonic forces, people can't afford to be careless. Careless people make the world more dangerous, and her job that much harder.

Hopefully—if Soto does the right thing—the threat of more demonic activity will be neutralized. As Lucy reaches the bottom of the staircase, she breathes a sigh of relief and tries to ignore how hot her amulet feels against her skin.

Her protective amulet is designed to pick up demonic presence, but it goes wild around George Soto. She thinks it must be because of all the demonic energy clinging to him, but she can't be sure; either way, it unsettles her. Whenever her amulet burns this hot, it usually means there's a demon around. She's far enough away from Soto that it should have cooled off by now.

She reaches for the door and feels a chill run down her back. Her eyes flicker over her shoulder, anxious. She is plagued by the familiar, skin-crawling sense of being watched. Try as she does to push it away, she can't ignore her gut.

Nothing is behind her. She faces an empty stairwell.

The doorknob turns and opens into a narrow corridor, illuminated by sterile fluorescent lighting. At the end of the hall, the steel door belies the freedom of outside. Lucy yearns for a breath of fresh air and finds her pace quickening as she makes her way down the hallway.

Some people are very, very foolish. George Soto is one of them, she decides. Putting himself in unnecessary danger for no reason—it's something she can't understand. Lucy prides herself on her caution. People willing to form a contract with a demon have no sense of self-preservation. Don't they understand how heavy the price of a contract is?

(She thinks she sees a flash of shadow out of the corner of her eye and forces herself to walk faster. The door is so close. Her necklace is burning.)

Lucy doesn't take unnecessary risks. She knows the value of her own soul. She has too much to live for to throw it away on foolishness.

(The hallway is growing narrower, darker. It's getting hard to breathe. Tendrils of smoke dance at the corners of her vision. The door is getting closer, closer, but it's still so far away.)

She's going to go home to Henry. They have plans for dinner again. She's going to listen to him tell her all about his day; she'll make up something that could have happened at the bookshop; they will share a bottle of wine, and giggle at each other over dessert. Home is safe; *Henry* is safe. She's going home.

(The door is getting farther and farther away. She tries to urge herself to walk, repeating her mantra of "shoulders back, eyes front," but Lucy's feet aren't moving anymore.)

There is a screaming in her ears, and dizziness bears down on her like rolling thunder.

Oh, she thinks, a fleeting thought amidst the blackness closing in on her mind. She won't be getting home to Henry after all. She hopes he won't wait up for her—

And, just like that, she is gone.

In the middle of the empty hallway, a broken amulet laying on the ground is the only sign anyone was ever there.

Chapter Seven

HIS HANDS ARE shaking as he struggles to light the match. He drags it across the side of the box, shooting a spark—but the flame doesn't catch. An acrid smell lingers in the air. George curses to himself as his hands continue to fumble. There's one last damn candle. He can do this.

Finally the match catches flame, and he holds it up long enough to bathe in the light. Fire dances at the tips of his fingers. Hastily, he lights the candle and blows the match out before he can be burned.

He shouldn't be doing this. Every ounce of his common sense is rebelling against summoning Jack again. The exorcist was in no way unclear about the consequences. Another summoning will make the "tear"—however big it already is—in the barrier worse. The demonic energy he's apparently dripping with will grow stronger; more opportunities will open up for things like whatever attacked poor Markieren to get through. By calling upon Jack again, George is putting more than his own life in danger.

If he had any other clue what to do, he'd stop this in its tracks; but George doesn't have another plan, he doesn't have a better idea. All he knows is that he needs to talk to Jack.

With the final candle lit, he returns to the familiar ritual. A drop of blood spills from his pricked finger as he reads out the familiar incantation. *"Ego adsum si vocare te voluntatem mea, serve meus, ad causam ego sto do tibi ius ego conjuro te factum est."*

He only has a few seconds to stumble out of the circle before the air grows thick, and shadows stretch to fill the room. The tug in his chest is nothing new this time; it is nowhere close to the blinding pain he had experienced when he first did this. Now the burn is almost familiar, a relief, like a bone setting back into place. It is as if being contracted to Jack is the way he is meant to exist.

Jack is disgruntled, but this is nothing new either. The mass of smoke that is his unsettled form rumbles, electricity dancing in front of George's eyes. "What the hell, George," he snarls. "I was doing something."

"Yeah," George agrees. His voice is tight, still hoarse from having his windpipe crunched; he sounds like a wreck, and must look just as bad. "You always are, aren't you, Jack? Is that why you couldn't answer your phone? I called you eight times."

A low rumble like thunder reverberates through the room. Jack wasn't expecting the harsh words, nor the icy tone he is greeted with. Any other day George might feel bad, but the betrayal churning within him overwhelms any sense of remorse. He feels himself choking on it with each breath. It takes all his self-restraint to keep himself from shouting, from demanding to know *why* and *how could he?* All he can do is glare. The demon before him seems to falter, if only for a second.

"I didn't have my phone," Jack says. He doesn't sound angry; if anything, he's cautious. It makes George's blood boil. "What's going on?"

"I dunno. How about you tell me?"

"Well, I've got no clue!" Jack snaps. "You dragged me here, and you're upset, so why don't you just tell me what happened—"

George raises his head, and the demon's voice cuts off abruptly. The candle flames cast his face into shadow, but the heavy bruising around his neck is still impossible to miss. For a second, George feels a twisted satisfaction as Jack falters under the shock. Then the mass of shadows grows dense, pressing inward until they have shifted into the form George knows so well. Jack's face reveals layers of shock, covered up with anger, barely masking alarm. All of the fear he won't allow his face to show shines from his dark eyes, wide as they take in George's condition.

Guilt strikes George like a punch to the stomach as Jack takes a step forward.

"What happened to your neck?"

George turns his head away, realizing too late that this only shows off the dark bruising around his throat. Jack moves closer to the boundaries of the circle, in spite of the force that keeps him confined within it.

"George, come on." Jack's own voice is low, a little dangerous. He sounds frightened too and doesn't have George's damn good excuse for it. "Who did that to you?"

"My boss," George replies. "Henry Markieren. I told you about him, remember? Only—it wasn't him, Jack. It wasn't him who did it."

"What the hell are you talking about?" Jack's hands clench into fists. "I'll kill him—"

"It wasn't him, Jack!" The sharpness is back along with the anger, and it spills out of George's mouth like poison. "There was something controlling him! A goddamn demon was controlling my boss, and you know why? He wanted to get to me. Apparently I'm some sort of demon magnet, because I've got all this energy all over me—hell, I'm pretty much swimming in the stuff."

He takes a step forward, gesturing wide around his apartment. "This entire place is crawling with it. You know why? It's all because of this! This summoning shit I've been doing! Come on, Jack, you've *got* to have known about that!"

He forces himself to pause, only to weigh Jack's reaction. When he sees it, something in his stomach curdles. It is impossible to mistake the guilt that mars Jack's face, darkening the eyes that never flicker from George's face. The sight of Jack's wordless confession stings more than hands around his throat ever could.

George huffs a breathless laugh. "Jesus, Jack."

"I kept telling you not to do it," Jack tells him. "You can't say I didn't try, George."

"No, that wasn't trying. That wasn't trying, because you knew I wasn't gonna listen to you. *Trying* would have been *telling* me that, hey, I'm putting a target on my own damn back by messing with this demon stuff. *Trying* would have been letting me know, warning me that I was screwing with some apocalyptic shit. But you didn't do that, did you, Jack?"

Jack says nothing. His stony eyes remain trained on George's face. George finds himself wishing he would just look away, because the longer those dark eyes pierce him, the more he can feel himself breaking.

"Why?" he demands, breathless. His words are tinged with more hurt than he wanted to face. "Why didn't you tell me?"

"I wanted to. I really did."

"Then why didn't you? Goddammit, Jack, what we're doing here is breaking things that aren't supposed to be touched!"

"I know that!" Jack shoots back, voice finally raising. It's cathartic to hear him yell; somehow, George feels a bit more in control.

"You never said anything to me. You never warned me, that every time I contracted you I was breaking open a literal door to hell! What would you have done if the damn tear actually broke, huh? If whatever shit you live with, whatever demons are going around possessing people and trying to kill people, got through? What if they hurt me?"

"I wouldn't have let that happen!"

"It almost did, Jack!" He sees the words strike Jack like a physical blow. "That night at the fair, you knew exactly what was going on!"

"That's a lie!"

"You saw me, you heard what happened, and you knew. How could you not have known? You knew it was dangerous, and that night something almost happened to me. Something did. What if it had been worse, huh? How would you have protected me?"

George can feel Jack's anger pulsating around the room, rolling over him like waves in a furious sea. They hit him like physical blows, but he doesn't buckle; he remains standing strong as Jack's eyes fill with blackness, as tendrils of smoke swirl in the circle around him. Jack's snarl shakes the walls. "You're *mine,* you belong to me! No one else can touch you! They can't—"

He falls silent. Eyes widen as he realizes what he's said; the darkness drains out of them at once, leaving them vulnerable and painfully human.

"George," he starts again, but George is beginning to understand what Jack's words meant.

"Jack," he says slowly, "what's the price of a contract?"

Jack says nothing. George has never seen Jack shrink, but that's the only word for what he does; it's a full-on retreat, cowering into himself as if he's afraid George will lash out and bite him. When Jack draws back, his walls go up. His expression closes off like a door slamming shut, and he draws himself to his full height to glower at George.

George can't go back; he can only press forward. "What happens when a contract is up? What's supposed to happen? What are the consequences, Jack?"

"Shut up, George," is all Jack growls, and George feels something in him snap.

"Tell me the price of a contract!"

It's a direct order. Just like that, the contract clicks into place, a sharp tug from inside George's ribs. Jack feels it too. His eyes widen as he realizes what George has done, but the other man is unfaltering. He continues to glower at Jack, pressing for the answer the demon's tongue compels him to give.

Jack has to swallow back the automatic instinct to reply; George watches the answer bob in his throat, words forced back down, before Jack's lips curl in a snarl.

"You don't get it, George," he says. "You don't know what you're doing."

George starts forward, no longer able to hold himself back; but his foot stumbles over the chalk line on the ground. It smudges, and there is a great rush of energy as the circle breaks. Jack takes a step back, and another, until he is outside of the bounds of confinement. His glare does not leave George's face.

"You really have no damn clue," he says, and then melts back into the shadows as if he was never there at all.

IT PROBABLY SAYS something about him that George's first instinct is to grab his phone.

There is a vice grip around his chest, and it is squeezing. He can't think past the toxic cocktail of despair and fury welling in his chest; he can't breathe through it. It fills up his lungs, threatening to drown him. It's not just Jack's lies. He is being overwhelmed by the slow-dawning certainty that he's done something horrible, something he can't go back from.

What happens when the contract's up?

Let's just say you're not my problem anymore.

What deal did he *make?*

His hands feel numb. His fingers fumble over the screen, barely able to unlock his phone, let alone find the number he needs. He presses dial and waits, the tight feeling in his chest increasing with every second.

"Soto!" crows a familiar voice over the line. "What's up, buddy? You are not gonna believe what happened at work today! I got a call from my boss's sister, and she was all upset because his wife—"

"Matt," George interjects, breathless. The tremor in his voice gives him away; Matt falls silent like he's been switched onto mute. "I—I need some help. I messed up."

Maybe it's the edge of urgency in his tone or the complete and utter panic that swirls beneath the surface leaking out through his words, but there isn't a second of hesitation. He can hear Matt shuffling from the other end of the phone line, and then he is all ears.

"Easy, George. Where are you?"

He takes a deep breath. "I'm at my apartment, but I— I'm getting out of here. Can you meet me?"

"Sure. Anything you need." In contrast to the sharp edge to George's tone, Matt keeps his voice relaxed and soothing. He sounds like he's trying to calm a frightened child or reassure a pet in the middle of a thunderstorm. In spite of himself, George can feel Matt's efforts working.

"I'll see you at the corner of French Street," he sighs, pulling a jacket over his shoulders. "There's something I've gotta do."

MATT DOESN'T COME alone, but George hasn't really expected him to. He's not surprised to pull the car door open to see Alex reclining against the window, with his legs splayed across the seat. Up in the passenger's seat, Josh offers him a mild salute. George shoved aside Alex's legs as he clambers in, and is rewarded with a light nudge to the thigh.

"What's with the scarf?" is the first thing out of Josh's mouth. Alex leans forward, curious, but George shoos him away. The bright red scarf wrapped around his neck is a stark contrast to the rest of his dark outfit, and out of place in the warm June weather. If he wants to hide the deep bruises around his neck, however, he needs it.

He hunches in on himself against the window, appreciating the feeling of constriction the seatbelt provides. He already feels painfully vulnerable; the last thing he wants is to spill out all his worries to his friends, who won't know how to handle it.

All he knows is that he can't be alone right now. He can't do this alone.

"Where to?" Matt asks. The words are on the tip of his tongue, but they won't come out. George only shrugs.

To Matt's credit, he only starts driving. A location would be appreciated, but it's not needed. He dodges traffic through downtown, past boutiques and playgrounds, around the local park where they all used to hide out and get drunk in college. The radio plays a slow indie tune, but it's mostly drowned out by Matt and Josh's conversation from the front. George isn't listening, but the background noise is appreciated all the same.

Alex doesn't contribute. He keeps watching, in that razor-sharp way he's always had. His eyes are a funny hazel-brown that don't match the deep mahogany of his skin; they stand out before he fixes them on you, but once he does, it's like being studied by a hawk. George has seen that gaze focused on professors and bosses before, but never on him. Alex is searching for an explanation in his closed-off demeanor, and it makes him feel like his every move is being scrutinized.

"Cut it out," he finally snaps, loud enough to throw the whole car into silence. Only the radio drones on, but it may as well be a hum of static. No one hears it, and no one cares. Everyone is looking at George.

Alex raises his eyebrows. After a few seconds, he turns his gaze away. George knows better than to think he's offended, or even perturbed.

"Okay," Matt finally says. "Now's the part where you tell us what's going on."

"Eyes on the road," George mutters, a bitter taste in his mouth. Matt rolls his eyes, turning back around just as the traffic light turns green.

"I'd like to know where I'm driving to."

"Yeah," pipes up Josh, voice loud to mask the anxiety swirling beneath its surface. "If I'm getting kidnapped, I wanna know where I'm going."

George sighs. The rush of air escapes him like air deflating out of a balloon. It doesn't take away any of the anxiety swirling within him, but the band of tension around his ribs loosens just enough for him to breathe. He takes a few deep inhales before he finally feels ready to speak.

"We've got to go back to the bookstore," he mutters. From his pocket, he pulls out a folded, crumpled piece of paper. Alex hisses as recognition clicks in his head, even before George unfolds it to reveal the stolen ritual page. "Things have gone wrong. Really wrong. I don't know how to make it better, but I've gotta keep it from getting worse. This is the only place I can think of."

Josh is staring at him like he's lost his mind. (George wonders if he hasn't.) "Are you insane?"

He shakes his head. "Honestly, I don't know."

"Damn it, Soto, first the demon thing and now this—"

"This is *all* about the demon thing," George spits. "This is all about the demon thing! Maybe they'll call the frickin' cops on me, maybe they won't. I don't know. But if they can help me, I need to try. Otherwise..."

Otherwise, I may have done something I can't fix. Otherwise I may have put the entire world at risk. Otherwise... otherwise I don't know what I've done to myself, but it might be something I can't go back on.

He doesn't know whether he can go back on what he's already done, but if the man from Lehexe's Books can tell him what he's done, then George doesn't have a choice.

Josh looks sick. Alex looks like he's not sure whether he wants to smack George or say "I told you so." Matt keeps his gaze trained on the road, not looking back.

After a painful moment's pause, George speaks again. "Look, I'm doing this with you guys or without you. I want you with me, though. I need you guys." His gaze flickers from Josh to Alex and finally to Matt's reflection in the rearview mirror. "What d'ya say? Are you in, or out?"

He still remembers the first day he met these guys: back in freshman year of college, none of them really sure where they fit in or what sort of people they were going to become. George was shorter than he was now, with thicker glasses and a bolder (if not smarter) mouth. Alex was a band geek. Josh was convinced he wanted to be a chef. Matt was eager to join every fraternity on campus and wound up joining none. By all rights, they never should have gotten along at all.

Still, they became friends. Something drew them to each other—a brotherhood that couldn't be broken by the worst of times. They've all been through some stormy weather, but they've dealt with it—as friends. That's what they've always done. They've had each other's backs, no matter what.

And hell, George knows how much he's asking for. He can only hope that same loyalty will stand, one last time.

For a long moment, no one speaks. George holds his breath, feeling apprehensive and hopeful all at once.

Finally, Alex heaves a sigh. He reaches out, clapping George on the shoulder. At once, a massive weight seems to fly from George's chest. He remembers how to take a breath again, how to think, and the relief is so great he could almost cry from it. There's resignation in his friend's eyes, but also a determination that shows no signs of faltering. When George turns to Josh, and then to Matt, he finds the same. Josh is smiling at him. There's an understanding in Matt's face, loyalty that is so familiar and so genuine that there's no mistaking it.

"To the end of the line, Soto," Alex says. George feels a smile break across his face.

"Well geez, guys," he laughs, feeling giddy for the first time today. "Let's not be sappy here, you know how emotional I get—"

His friends roll their eyes and spit back their own retorts. George finds himself chuckling. Even for a second, it feels like everything could be all right after all.

BY THE TIME they pull up in front of Lehexe's Books, George's heart is beating a frenetic samba in his chest. He's still got the ritual clasped in his closed hand. The paper feels as if it burns his skin. As much as he'd like to tuck it back into his pocket or drop it, he cannot; that feels inexplicably like he is abandoning his own actions. He was the one who stole the spell. He was the one who summoned Jack, over and over again. He needs to own the responsibility of his own sins.

He does not put the paper away. As the car jerks to a stop outside the store, he clutches his fingers more tightly around it, causing the paper to crinkle.

The shop looks different in the daytime. The outside is just as George remembers it, small and classical, with wide bay windows cluttered with books. It is much different in the daytime, however. The sense of surreality that existed past dark has vanished with the sun, leaving only an echo of it whispering in the back of George's mind. The ominous-ness that lingered from that night has gone, too. George is able to walk up the cobblestone sidewalk with only the slightest hint of unease, and that's because he knows what he's about to walk into.

When he was six, his attention was caught by a plastic wind-up figurine while his mother was paying for groceries. She led him out of the store hand-in-hand. George was so eager to help her load the grocery bags into the car, and then the house, that he didn't remember he slipped the windup toy into his pocket until later that night.

George still remembers setting that tiny plastic frog on his bedroom floor, winding it up, and watching it jump. The thrill he got from seeing his ill-won prize dance around his room could not be compared to anything he experienced before or since. There is something electrifying about holding something that should not belong to you in your hand, and knowing it's yours anyway.

George never stole anything after that day—not until the spell. Enticed as he was by the exhilaration of a caper, the risk of getting caught was always too great. George was the sort of kid who cracked jokes in class and got into verbal fistfights on the playground. He never put himself in a position to get in real trouble, especially legal trouble—and this caution carried into adulthood.

Now, he's about to march into that shop and *turn himself in* as a thief. It's the only thing he can do, but it goes against every instinct in his body.

He stops just outside the door, hand hesitating over the doorknob. What the hell is he doing?

"George," prompts Alex, and George swallows hard. There's only one thing he can do.

If he wants a chance at understanding any of this—what he's done, and more importantly, how to keep it from getting worse—he needs help. He needs someone who knows what on earth is going on.

He can't think of anyone else who might have a clue. The bookstore owner is his only shot.

"Right," he says, and takes a deep breath. His eyes squeeze shut for just a second. "Right," he repeats and pushes open the door. A bell over the entrance chimes as he steps into the shop.

Everything seems similar to how he last saw it, if not perfectly exact. He couldn't expect it to be. The clutter of papers covering the counter obviously could not stray. Now the counter is clear, glistening mahogany wood ready to greet a set of customers. The floor is neater, stacks of books pushed off into far corners. The door behind the counter—leading to the bathroom, and who knows where else—is shut.

The most striking difference, however, is the person behind the counter. They definitely aren't the guy George remembers from their midnight visit. In fact, they're not a *guy* at all.

The woman behind the counter is as unfamiliar to George as the shop is familiar. She, too, seems as if she does not quite fit into this plane of reality. There is a dreamlike quality to her that allows her to blend in with the rest of the shop perfectly. Her hands do not seem to fall upon the keys of the cash register; to George's distracted mind, they look like they're dancing.

Her head raises to meet them, and a pearly smile lights up her face. George is struck by how pretty she is, in an antique sort of way that perfectly fits the shop around her. She's got a face like an old-time Gibson Girl, round gray eyes, a delicately sloped nose, and a heart-shaped jawline that makes her smile all the more pronounced. Her brown hair hangs to her shoulders, loose around her face, and she has some strands pulled behind her head, presumably to keep them out of her face. There is no name tag on her clothes. She could work here, or she could just as easily be a woman who wandered in, stepped behind the counter, and decided to set up shop.

This seems unlikely a second later, when she shuts the register and beams at the newcomers. "Hello," she greets, in a voice laced with a light accent. "Welcome! Are you looking for anything in particular?"

George's hand still lingers over his pocket; he can feel the paper crinkle through the layer of thin denim. He hesitates, then sticks his hand into his pocket instead. He hopes the gesture looks casual; it probably doesn't.

"Uhh—" Josh, as always, finds himself rendered stupid around a beautiful woman. That doesn't keep him from running his mouth anyway. "We're looking for a guy, actually. Tall, black, kinda gloomy, probably runs the place, if you know him—"

"We have a few questions for him," Alex interjects, giving Josh a sharp elbow in the ribs. "Is he around?"

"You're looking for Adam." The woman nods knowingly, looking a little apologetic. "He's busy in the back right now. I can try to answer any questions you have."

"I'm not sure that's—" Matt starts, but is cut off when George suddenly steps up to the desk.

"I need to talk to Adam. I've got to give him something," he says, slapping his palm down in front of the woman. Her eyes flicker from the crinkled spell paper beneath it, then back up to him. Slow as a statue remembering how to move, she nods her head.

"Adam. Come out here, please?"

The pitch of her voice carries through the closed door behind the cash register. It takes a second, but the sound of another door closing echoes from the back, and then a deeper voice yells, "Be right there!"

"Where did you find this?" the woman demands in the meantime, staring at George hard. It is impossible not to squirm under her scrutiny.

"I took it. I-It was an accident, okay?"

"An accident?" the woman demands and barks a short laugh. "That's what they're calling theft these days?"

"I didn't mean to steal from you!"

"What's goin' on here?"

The sudden new voice slices through the room's tension like a water over a fire. It is smooth and deep, a complete contrast to the whirring chaos of George's own thoughts. He goes still in an instant. When he straightens up, he is not surprised to be met with the bookstore owner's face.

"Adam," the woman says; and in a lower, tighter voice, "the *spell*." This just confirms what George feared—that they know the spell was missing, and have been *looking for it.*

The girl fires off a string of words in rapid French; the sound makes George's head spin. Adam steps up to her, brow furrowed, and shakes his head. She grows more insistent, gesturing at them, and Adam responds in a cool tone—a complete counter to George's swirling anxiety.

"Il est celui qui l'a pris! Qui sait ce qu'il a fait?"

"Je doute qu'il sache," Adam replies, eyes locking on George. *"Il a peur."*

It's obvious that they're talking about him. George offers a tiny wave, which neither of the shopkeepers seem to appreciate. Adam takes a step forward, hands in the pockets of his washed-out jeans. "So *that's* where my spell went."

George swallows. "I took it by accident that night. I swore it was a prank—some sort of joke book, a Halloween thing. It seemed too crazy to be real, you know?"

"You usually find Halloween decorations in the middle of autumn. Not during summer, in a stack of other books, that someone's clearly been working on. If you'd done a bit of research, you might have realized how real it is."

George hangs his head. He can feel the gazes of his friends burning into his back; it stings even more than Lucy's piercing green eyes had when she decried his stupidity. The woman has her arms crossed, stern and angry, while the bookstore owner just looks exasperated.

There is exhaustion lining his face, as if he's seen more than his share of late work nights; behind the thin frame of his glasses, heavy bags sit beneath his eyes. Still, he has enough energy to step around the counter and lean back on it, shaking his head. He studies George like a hawk studies a mouse. George feels trapped under his scrutiny.

"Just tell me, did you do the ritual?" George opens his mouth to reply, but Adam cuts him off. "How *many times* did you do the ritual?"

Behind him, Josh coughs. George shoots his friend an uncharitable look before turning back to Adam, shamefaced. "It might have been more than once or twice."

Adam raises his eyebrows.

"Okay, four times. Five. Maybe—*maybe* six?"

"Oh my goodness." The woman presses a hand to her forehead, voice strained. Her shoulders heave with short peals of laughter that sound more like sobs. "You have to be kidding me."

"Sophie," Adam sighs, and the woman silences herself. She returns to the counter, snatching a book from the top of a small pile on the floor, and begins to tear through it as if she's searching for something. Adam doesn't spare Sophie another glance. All of his attention is focused on George and the paper in his hand.

"Look, whatever he did, we can fix it, right?" Matt suddenly speaks up from behind his friend. When all eyes turn to him he shrinks, a little uncertain, but stands his ground.

"I'm afraid it's not that simple," Adam answers levelly.

"Come on, it can't be that bad. Right?"

"Your friend might have created a tear between worlds that could put all of Earth at risk."

Alex's jaw drops open. Josh makes a strangled noise in the back of his throat. Matt just winces. "Oh."

George has already gotten this lecture from Lucy, and he doesn't need to hear it again. "I know I messed up, okay? I know what I did. I just have to know how to fix it."

"There's no way to fix what you did," Adam retorts, crossing his arms. "It's not like you stabbed a hole in drywall and you can just repair it with some plaster. The barrier is a living, breathing thing. It's not sentient, but it's got a life force all its own, and it can feel when something's wearing it out. If it gets tired enough, it'll rip—and I'd say you've damn near exhausted it."

"This explains the spike in demonic energy around town these past few days," Sophie says in a rush, face still buried in her book. "My psychic friend mentioned that Lawrence Street is practically drowning in it."

"That's where I live," George says in a weak voice. Sophie rolls her eyes.

"*That* explains it." She curls her pink lips back; a tiny grunt escapes her as her rapid page-turning slices one of her fingers.

"The tear will repair itself over time, if you let it. Until then, there's nothing else you can do. This is the only way to keep your stupidity from turning into a crisis." Adam frowns down his nose at George. Slowly, the harshest edges of the scowl melt from his face. They are replaced by something thoughtful. It takes George a moment to recognize it for what it is: *worry.*

Concern and curiosity plays across his face in equal measure; George wonders what the man can read from his own distraught expression. Finally, Adam sighs. "Cleanse yourself. Cleanse your home. Use clear crystals and sage, maybe some sandalwood incense. Pray that you haven't already caused enough damage that something can get through."

He takes a step closer and reaches out, plucking the paper from George's stiff hands. "And for the love of sanity," he tells him. "Do *not* summon any more demons."

George swallows hard, blinking back into those cool, solemn eyes. There is sympathy etched into the crease of his brows. Adam has a face that could easily be called handsome, if he didn't look so strung out. George is reminded of the expression a concerned parent would wear, rather than a stranger. The fact that this man he doesn't know, this man he's stolen from, is so concerned about him that he won't even waste time being angry. Something about that chills George more than he can comprehend.

"Be careful, George," Adam bids, in a voice too low for anyone else to hear. "Keep a tight grip on your soul."

George draws away, eyes wide—but no more answers are forthcoming. Adam lowers his head and turns away, paper clutched tight in his hands. He tucks it back into a nearby book, where it becomes one of the mess of papers pressed within. The ritual is safe; but George has the awful, settling certainty that he is not.

He feels a hand lock on his shoulder. "Come on, buddy, we've gotta go," Josh urges. "George. Come on."

George releases a shuddering breath, and forces himself to turn his back on the shop and its scornful owners. He's done all he can here. There is nothing more to say.

One after another, his friends file out of the shop. They return to Matt's car, frown out the windows as they begin to move down the street, and try furiously not to think about what the shop owner told them.

It's next to impossible. Adam's low warning rings in George's head, an ominous chorus, only frowning louder the farther he is carried away. *Be careful, George,* he recalls. His lips twist into a bitter smile. There's one thing he's never been good at.

It's only after they've left the bookshop well behind them that George realizes why he cannot escape the icy feeling in the pit of his stomach: he never told Adam his name.

Chapter Eight

THEY WIND UP going to the bar afterward. Most of the nights they get together they end up at the bar. Tonight, as unorthodox as it is, is no different. Whether they go out of genuine desire for camaraderie, or just a need for something constant, something familiar, George couldn't say.

Whatever the reason, and no matter if he's in a state to enjoy himself or not (stunningly, he isn't) he finds himself slumped over a table at Larkin's bar that night, with Matt and Josh across from him and Alex pressed against his side.

A cloud of silence hangs over the group. It is as unnatural as it is uncomfortable. George cannot remember a time his friends were ever gloomy. Even in the midst of finals, through the storms of bad breakups and campus clashes, their group has never let negativity drive a wedge between them.

Things are different now. George cannot help wondering if *everything* is different now.

He looks around at the faces of his friends, hunched over their drinks, and his stomach twists. He feels miles away from them; he cannot force himself to even try to reach out.

How could he, when this is all his fault? He started this mess in the first place, and now it's becoming clear just how badly he's screwed up.

He assumed that by summoning Jack, he was affecting himself and only himself. He never knew what he was doing at all. He never gave consideration to how the demon world worked, the rules of whatever metaphysical magic was allowing him to contact Jack in the first place—hell, he didn't even think about the people living next door. It was his apartment, right? His life?

How could he have been so ignorant? Of course it wouldn't only affect him. It affected everything around him—he was like a walking hurricane, the center of a storm that no one could even see. Now the shadows he kept seeing from the corner of his eye make sense. His cat's strange behavior is no longer a mystery. The way his mood has dropped in the past few weeks, shifting from happy to mercurial in the blink of an eye....

That night at the fair...

Did Jack know then? Could he have told George what was happening to him, what was going on? The image of Jack's face, shadowed with worry and *something else* floats back into his mind. Of course he knew. He knew exactly what was going on.

The worst part is, he cared for Jack. Past the lust-driven attraction he felt at their first meeting, he'd gotten to know Jack and care for him. He stopped seeing him as "the demon" and started seeing him as Jack—who never uses emojis, who hates anything but pepper on his pizza, who gets queasy from heights and fast roller coasters, but who thinks bumper cars are the coolest. Jack, who made him laugh without trying, and who let George squirm past his well-fortified walls. George opened himself up to Jack, and he felt as if Jack had done the same.

Does he love Jack? He thinks he did.

He loved him before he knew he *lied* to him. Every time George summoned him, he was opening a door a little bit wider, and Jack knew it. Still, he let him. Time after time, he appeared in George's apartment and grumped at him for summoning him, but he never tried to stop him. Not really. He never told him what could be happening, even when he saw it firsthand.

Jack knew and kept it from him.

George doesn't understand why.

Whatever Jack's motives, he's still the idiot who put the world at risk. He summoned Jack time after time, even after he knew how dangerous it was. Anything that could happen now is on his shoulders. That guilt is his alone to bear.

Swirling his beer, George studies his reflection in the amber liquid and tries not to wince. His hair is uncombed, hanging ragged in his face. The scarf around his neck is anything but inconspicuous, given it's a hot June night and the bar's air conditioning is practically nonexistent. His glasses are crooked. He looks as bad as he feels, which is saying something.

His poor mood is contagious. It affects the rest of the party, like an anchor on a sinking ship. Matt and Josh are keeping a running dialogue about nothing much, and trying to engage the rest of the group; but they're as subdued as everyone else, and it shows.

George's instinct is to say something to lighten the mood, but he's got nothing; every time he opens his mouth, he can only grimace. Everything seems inappropriate right now, and he's coming up blank. Being unable to be himself is the worst thing. He knows who he is—he's the clown, the one who keeps everybody's spirits up, who doesn't let things get to him. That's his role to play, and he plays it well. When he can no longer do that...

He shouldn't be here. He's even put his friends at risk with this whole disaster, and now he's ruining his friends' night. He's the last thing they need right now.

"Sorry," he says distractedly, after yet another attempt to engage him in the conversation sails over his head. Matt is leaning forward, face open and questioning, but George hasn't heard a word he's said all evening. "I shouldn't be out. It's... a bad night. Sorry, guys, I'm gonna go."

"No. Hang on." Matt reaches out to him. George's instinct is to flinch away, but he's trapped in the booth and Alex is blocking him in. He couldn't get out of his seat even if he wanted to, and he's only half sure he does. Being out here is bad, but being alone with his thoughts would be worse.

As usual, Matt can read him like a book. "You *really* sure that being alone is what you want right now?"

George's eye twitches. Damn Matt, always too perceptive for his own good. "No. I'm honestly not. But I don't feel like I should be out here."

"You said that. Why?"

George tries to squirm out of his seat, but the table blocks him in. The only way out of the booth is to go under the table, and George isn't that desperate. Yet.

"It's my fault, okay? I screwed up and didn't think about the consequences. Typical George, right?" he offers a short laugh; it dies as it's met by his friends' humorless faces. George wilts ever further, which he hadn't realized was possible. "Look, I'm not in a great place. I don't want to drag you guys down with me."

"So you're going back home," Josh says flatly.

"What's it matter, guys?" In lieu of escape, he tosses back another long drink of beer. When he pulls back, he can't help wincing—he needs something stronger. "It's just... just me. I should have listened." To Alex, when he warned him not to mess with the spell; to Jack, who kept telling him not to summon him; to his own damn instincts. "I shouldn't have done what I did. But I did it, and now things are messed up, and people—I just…" He swallows, thinking of Markieren's face; of Jack's. "I just don't want anyone to get hurt."

His friends can understand that. A round of unreadable looks pass around the group before Matt sighs.

"Stay here," he beseeches, earnest as ever in the face of what he sees as a friend in need. (George doesn't need *anything* except for a new apartment and enough hard liquor to put him to sleep for six months.) He reaches across the table, laying a hand on his shoulder, and his touch grounds George like an anchor.

Matt's blue eyes are wide; his face looks young, honest, determined. George could leave, and knows he probably should, but he is wanted here. His friends want him, and that makes all the difference.

Alex's words from the car echo in George's head. *To the end of the line, huh?*

"All right," he concedes, slamming a hand down on the tabletop. "Who's buying shots?"

A round of cheers resounds from the table. It's far from their usual enthusiasm, but also the most alive they've been all night. George feels a rush of relief at seeing smiles light up his buddies' faces once more. He endures the pats on the back and exclamations of "Atta boy, Soto!" with feigned exasperation, but can't keep the smirk off his own face.

Matt slaps a handful of bills on the table. "What's everyone want? Vodka? Whiskey? Some fruity shit no one can pronounce the name of?"

"Ethanol," George deadpans. Matt and Josh exchange wide-eyed looks before Josh says, loudly, "Tequila sounds great!"

Only when he's got three shots of tequila in his bloodstream does George finally start to come to life again. Like a man waking from sleep, or a statue turning from stone to flesh, he begins to see the world around him as more than a shadowy landscape. Colors are sharp, sounds are loud, and George can breathe again without feeling like his throat is being crushed.

"It's such a bastard move, you know," he rambles, even though he's not quite sure what he's saying. "Like, you don't *lie* to a person. Someone who cares about you. You think— you think somebody gives half a shit about you, then hey, turns out they don't. Instead, they're a demon. Like, a literal fucking demon. I mean, I *knew* that, but still. It's not fair. It isn't fucking fair."

No one seems to know how to approach the "friend has broken up with his demon" thing. No one tries. Alex, at least, makes an effort to empathize. "I feel you, man." He claps George on the back, a little harder than necessary. George sways. Then again, that could be the tequila. "When Maria broke up with me, I had no clue what I was doing. I didn't know where I was all night. Literally. She broke up with me on a train, and then I forgot to get off. I got lost."

Matt sets his empty shot glass down with a clink. "Sounds like a 'you' problem, Al."

Alex hums his agreement, still sulking over memories of his last ex-girlfriend. He's distracted momentarily by George; his eyes catch on his friend, and then the scarf still wrapped around his neck.

"Okay, seriously. The scarf. What's the deal?"

Before he can stop him, Alex reaches over and seizes the end of the scarf wrapped around George's neck.

"Hey, hands to yourself," George fires back, ducking out of the way. His hands fly up to re-secure his protection, and he shoots Alex a glare that's only half playful. "What's with the hair?"

Alex touches his own head of springy dark curls, expression twisting. "What's with the glasses?"

"What's with the face?"

"What's with the shitty comebacks?" Josh asks with an exaggerated groan, setting his phone down on the table. "Kiss and make up or start hitting each other. If I've got to listen to a second more of this, *I'll* hit you."

"Can't expect much else, going out with you guys," shoots back Alex. "Regular geniuses, every one of us."

George holds up a finger. "Einsteins. We're Einsteins."

"Sure are brilliant at cheering you up, though," Matt remarks, reaching for another shot. He looks up at George, victory dancing in the gleam of his eyes. "Look at you. You're smiling already."

George swipes a hand across his mouth and, sure enough, finds a grin there. He's surprised. He hadn't realized his foul mood had faded so easily, but the combination of alcohol and his friends worked like magic. He exhales in a single breath, allowing himself to soak in the relief of his own smile. He was right in seeking out company tonight.

Matt's own lips curl upwards in a catlike beam. "I guess this makes us regular experts in *'cheering George up,'* huh?"

"We deserve medals," chimes Josh. "Big ones. Shiny."

"A presidential commendation," Alex adds, elbowing George. "You're a pain sometimes."

Matt chuckles, leaning back in his seat. "Yup. We're the best damn friends—"

And then it happens.

George doesn't see it coming. He doesn't get a chance to see more than the curve of Matt's grin; the flash of Josh's golden eyes; the sleeve of Alex's checkered shirt brushing against his arm. He hears something behind him that sounds like a roar, but there is no time to think, to question, to fear.

And then—

Everything—

Gone.

WHEN GEORGE NEXT comes back to himself, he is on the ground. He can make out that much, because the floor is hard against his ribs and something is digging into his thigh, but he doesn't know what is going on until he forces his eyes to open. As soon as they do, he wants to snap them shut again. Everything is so bright, and the ringing in his ears is too much to think through. Nausea is overwhelming; he picks up his head, gags, but brings nothing up before he collapses back down again.

What he can make out of the world swirls around him in a dizzying landscape. He gradually becomes aware of more than the pounding in his head and the ringing in his ears. He feels the heat that screams fire, close to him, too close. He hears someone sobbing, another voice raised in a shrill scream. He hears footsteps, roaring, thunder—

FLASH.

There was an explosion. He realizes this as he forces himself to raise his head again. The world blew up—no, no, the *bar* blew up, so close to where they were sitting that he could feel the concussion rolling over his body.

Now, crumpled on the ground, everything hurts. He must have broken something; there is an agony in his chest, and something shifts when he moves in a way that makes him scream. He's been thrown clear across the room, he realizes. His back is against what remains of the bar, his body is crumpled, and something warm runs down the side of his face.

His gaze swivels around the room, pushing past the dizziness to search for something, anything, that makes sense.

"M-Matt," he chokes out, and can't hear his own voice. "Josh? Alex!"

They're gone. He can't see his friends anywhere. He can't see anything. It's so dark down here, why is it so *dark—*

When he feels something spill onto his back, his eyes are drawn up automatically. He is confronted with a wall of multicolored bottles, shattered and dripping, many of them barely holding themselves onto their shelves. It takes a few seconds of dazed blinking before he realizes that it's alcohol raining onto him, along with shards of glass. He was thrown clean behind the bar.

The smell of smoke is heavy now, wispy above George's head. He forces himself up on his knees and elbows, recognizing the necessity of moving. He has to go, now.

Broken glass splinters beneath him as he crawls out from behind the bar. He feels it dig into his skin, cutting him, but he forces himself not to focus on it. He needs to keep going—his friends are here somewhere, and they all need to get out. He sees a figure rush past him, past the flames steadily creeping across the floor and walls and hears a scream of someone who isn't as lucky. Debris dominates the ruined bar; splintered wood and broken glass litter the floors, broken tables are everywhere, and unmoving shapes remain slumped on the ground. George's head spins as he focuses on these figures; a rush of alarm hits him at the realization that they're bodies.

People—broken, hurt, and bleeding—on the ground. Not moving.

His friends' names tear from his lips again, and he forces himself over to the nearest unmoving form. He seizes the body and flips it over, only to reveal an unfamiliar face. The man's eyes are open, wide and unseeing. A small whimper escapes George as he lets the body go.

"George!"

The shout slices through his horror, and he spins around too fast. Dizziness catches up with him all at once. He slumps forward, vision blacking out, but before he can hit the ground he is caught up in strong arms.

"No—stay with me, oh my God, don't pass out, *shit—*"

George forces his eyes open again to take in an ash-streaked face. The ginger hair is unmistakable, but those eyes are wide with more panic than George has ever seen. Josh looks absolutely terrified.

"Are you bleeding? Oh my God. George, what do I do—"

"Where are the guys?" George forces out, blinking in a desperate attempt to clear his head. "Where are they?"

"I don't know—I don't know, something exploded and we all went flying, I don't know what it was—"

"Josh." George grabs his friend's shoulder, and the back of his mind registers it as hilarious that he's comforting someone right now. Then again, this is his second near-death experience in a day—he's becoming a pro. His gesture must have the right effect, because Josh forces a few deep breaths through his lungs and nods his head.

"You gotta move with me, George," he says. "We've gotta find Matt and Alex."

George's eyes turn to the bodies on the ground once more, and he feels a vice of panic lock around his chest. If one of those is Matt or Alex, are they even still alive?

"I think—" George starts, but is cut off by the sound of a scream.

It isn't like any scream he's ever heard before. He's heard screams of astonishment, of alarm, of laughter. He's heard screams of absolute terror. He's heard Sawyer scream as he tore through the office pursued by a demon, he's heard Matt scream at his surprise party last year, he's heard his little sister scream when she broke her arm. This scream is on a completely different level than any that George has heard before.

It is a scream of someone who is about to die.

George knows this in his bones a second before he turns to the source, and his eyes land on the corner of the burning room. A strangled sound escapes his throat as he recognizes the mass of smoke, a very familiar mass of smoke he has seen more than once before.

It's the same smoke that came out of Markieren's mouth. It's the same smoke that's appeared in his living room every time he's contracted Jack.

It's a demon, bearing down on a panic-stricken Alex.

George lurches forward at the second the entity descends on Alex, swallowing him up in blackness. His final scream is cut off by a great roaring that fills the entire room, rattling the walls and causing the fire to flicker. It's like the sound of a blender—tearing something apart all at once, destroying it. George is thrown back into Josh, who is thrown back against a splintered booth, and they hunch together in horror until the roar dies away.

When they raise their heads again, the only thing left in the spot where Alex was is carnage. There's so much blood that George could swim in it; enough blood to fill a bathtub, enough blood to drown a man. He never knew there was that much blood in a human body.

"Where is it?" he screams over Josh's howls of their friend's name. "Where did it go?"

The demon did that. George never knew a demon could do that.

"Oh God—" Josh is gripping hold of him now like a lifeline. George can feel his own pulse pounding in his ears. Each blink sends Alex's last expression flashing back into his mind, the screaming and the blood. He wants to gag again but can't bring himself to move.

Thunder roars in his ears again.

His eyes open to blackness, and he lifts his head just in time to see that the demon has reappeared. It is writhing over their heads, bearing down on them, and all George can see is black, black, black.

Destruction in its emptiness, death in its hollow core. Each pulse makes him sick, each inch closer crushes him. He knows now what Alex felt when he was screaming. There is no hope of escape, not as the entity presses down on top of them, so close to consuming them whole that every breath George takes is a lungful of sulfur.

He squeezes his eyes shut before he hears the yell.

"Come over here!"

The voice is instantly familiar. George's eyes shoot open wide, and Josh's gaze swivels away from the screeching Death above them to seek out its source. There is no one else who can strike the pulse of their hearts so soundly; no one else whose voice they were minutes ago desperate to hear.

Matt is hunched at the other end of the room, crouched against the burning bar. He is heedless of the cinders falling onto his head; his focus is entirely on George and Josh, arms outstretched and beckoning to them. There is an intensity on his face, earnestness mixed with desperation, and that same lionhearted fearlessness Matt only ever shows in the thick of real danger.

The demon's attention is distracted. George wonders if it is the life radiating from Matt at every angle, or just that he shouted so loudly. Matt is still gesturing his friends to apparent safety when the demon begins to back off them, shifting its attention towards the other side of the room.

Matt sees it coming, but his gaze does not stray from George and Josh. His arm is still extended, stretching towards them in desperation.

"Come on! Over here! Over here!"

Does he know he will die? Does he see Death coming for him, swooping down with black claws outstretched? Did he know all along that shouting would sign his own death warrant, or does he realize it when he sees the mass descending? Does he realize it at all? In the moment before it consumes him, *does Matt know?*

Or, all along, is he really calling out for his friends to join him in safety?

He screams again. *"Over here!"*

The black shadow swallows him up.

This time there is no dying wail for the demon's roar to drown out. There is nothing but the thunder in George's ears, all around him, everywhere. The walls rattle, debris rains down, and when the demon moves away there is nothing left of Matt to reach out to.

The shriek that tears from Josh's throat is more animal than human. George is screaming too, he knows, but he cannot hear himself. Only the burn in his throat and his heart pounding hard enough to burst out of his chest reassures him he is still alive.

The demon's attention turns back to them again, and he realizes he won't be for much longer.

I don't want to die, he thinks to himself. *I want to live. I want to* live.

Matt and Alex probably wanted to live too. Josh's fingers dig into his arms, piercing flesh. George closes his eyes as shadows descend upon him once more.

And then—

Nothing.

He doesn't know what he expects—a blinding agony, maybe, the sensation of being torn apart... but it doesn't come. He opens his eyes to brightness, blinding, burning *brightness* which makes him fight not to shut them again.

He knows immediately that the being standing in front of them is not the same demon who attacked them seconds ago. This creature is pure white-hot fire, pulsating with energy so strong it makes George lightheaded. He cannot stare for too long before his eyes begin to burn. The one thing he can make out, clearer than anything else in the chaos inside his head and around him, is the fact that the creature is shielding them.

Its arms are outstretched, its legs are spread, and it is blocking the demon's access to the two cowering men. Like a guardian angel, it is keeping them from further harm.

"Holy shit," is all George is able to mumble before a concussion blast tears from the light entity's body. He feels it hit him, recoils back as his head seems to shatter into a million pieces, and he doesn't get the chance to think before his world goes dark.

WHEN HE OPENS his eyes again, the first thing he feels is warmth.

"Hey," greets Jack, from where he hovers inches above George's own face. There is a gentleness to his expression that George has never seen before; a softness, a knit to his brow which belies anxiety he refuses to show. When George opens his eyes further Jack's lips twitch in a small smile.

"How you feeling?" he asks, voice soft.

George tries to form words, but his tongue feels thick. He manages a groan, then another as he struggles to sit up. Jack is right there, hand behind his neck to support him as he helps prop George up against the wall behind him.

It's a brick wall, George realizes hazily. They're in a dark alleyway; the air is free of smoke; the stars glimmer bright in the sky above them; and the fire is gone.

"Where are we?" he manages to ask.

"A few blocks away. I brought you both here. Everything's fine, George. You're gonna be okay."

George wants to believe him, but his mind is filled with images of blood and devastation. "'M I hurt? Hurt bad?"

"No way. A few broken ribs, a concussion, maybe, but you're okay. I've got you. Everything's gonna be fine. I'm here."

Jack keeps repeating himself. This stands out to George because Jack rarely—if ever—repeats himself. He also never rambles, so the fact that he is now means he must be more shaken up than he's willing to admit. Why would he be so shaken up, unless....

"You saved us," George realizes, gaping at Jack's face. Even after their argument earlier, Jack has still come to his protection when he needed it most. "Jack, you... oh my God. Josh."

George's attention snaps to the alley around him, and he only has to search for a few moments before he sees him—Josh, ash-streaked and very still, hunched over on top of a garbage can.

The sight of his friend makes George feel nauseated, not just because seeing Josh so subdued feels wrong. There is no glow to him, no spark of life as bright as fire *(fire burning down Larkin's bar, fire haloing Matt's head as he called out to them)*. Josh looks half dead, and the thought brings flashes to George's mind—Alex's dying scream, Matt's last wide-eyed look.

He slumps forward with a whimper and rasps out his friend's name. Josh doesn't look up; he's muttering to himself, staring down at his hands as tears stream down his cheeks. George forces himself to focus on the words that leave halting lips.

"Oh, God... God, oh God, oh..."

Josh is cradling something in his hands—a flash of silver, singed with smoke and malformed by fire. It takes a few seconds of peering at the twisted metal for realization to descend upon George like a shock of icy water. It's Matt's engagement ring. How Josh got it George doesn't know, but he cradles it now like a lifeline.

In a way, it *is*. This is all they have left of Matt. It is their only proof he was ever there to begin with.

"He's gone," Josh whimpers. "They're gone. They're both gone."

"I—" George starts, but his voice chokes up in a sob. He tries forcing himself out of Jack's grip to stand, but his legs give out on him all at once. He's falling before he can even think about hitting the ground. The only thing that saves him are Jack's arms locking around him, solid and grounding as George feels himself begin to drift off to a faraway place.

"Jack." He looks up at the demon, desperate. "Tell me this didn't happen 'cause of me."

"George—"

"Tell me! *Please*."

Jack looks anguished. "I can't, George. I don't know, I can't. I'm sorry."

George buries his face in the demon's chest. There are no tears; he doesn't cry. George remains very, very still, and allows Jack to hold him as if he is the only thing left in the world.

Chapter Nine

THINGS ARE QUIET.

After everything that happened, it is a relief to be back in a place where things almost make sense again. George doesn't feel quite so lost, sitting in the middle of his apartment. He can breathe again, and that's something. Even if his head is still reeling and he can hear screams echoing in his ears, at least he's home.

Jack is the one who carries him there. Exhaustion leaves George dozing in Jack's arms, so he doesn't remember much about the way they got home; he doesn't remember Jack setting him on the couch, undressing him and wrapping a blanket around him. He doesn't remember the look on Jack's face as he pressed a glass of water into George's hands, urging him to drink something. He doesn't remember Jack's calloused hands running over each of his injuries, fingertips knitting skin, setting bone, and leeching the pain away.

George's first clear memory, once he's come back to what he'd almost call consciousness, is waking up the next morning laying on top of Jack's chest.

The television is on, a dull drone in the background. George's attention, however, is elsewhere. He is keenly aware of the muscular chest he is pillowed against; of the arms holding him; of the hand stroking slowly up and down his back, while the other runs through his hair. It takes him a minute to realize the vibrations that woke him in the first place is Jack singing.

He's got a low voice, rich with smoky undertones that seem to smolder just underneath his rasp. The sound is soothing; George could lie here and listen to it forever if given the chance. All songs come to an end, however, and he waits for Jack to finish his before giving away the fact that he's awake.

"I didn't know you could sing."

"I like the song," is all Jack says. He seems a bit embarrassed about it. This fades away to relief as George shifts up all on his own and looks around, dazed but aware. "How're you feeling?"

"Mmm. Shitty," George mutters, and presses a hand to his head. "Feels like I have the worst hangover in the world."

Jack reaches for him, and fingertips gloss over his forehead. A blissful numbness fills the cracks of George's brain—it's like someone's injected him with ice water, forcing him to go limp as all the pain is seeped away at once. He inhales a breath and gets lightheaded again, only to be steadied by Jack's hands.

"You just woke up on me. Don't go out again so soon, okay?"

George shakes his head to clear it and turns away from Jack to begin taking stock of himself. The awful agony in his chest from last night is gone; so is the piece of glass that was buried in his thigh, the burns on his hands and legs, and even the soreness in his throat. When he touches the skin of his neck, it doesn't hurt. He's willing to bet there is no bruise left behind.

"You could'a told me you could heal stuff earlier. Would have saved me a lot of aches and pains."

"You walk into another glass door, it's your problem," Jack retorts. The sound of his dry humor makes George exhale, too overwhelmed with shock and relief to even attempt a smile. His head still feels cloudy. It's more than that familiar post-nap haze—this is something deeper, more emotional than physical, a numbness similar to Jack's pain-relief. He half-wonders if Jack did something to freeze the shock and loss where it stands in George's chest, heavy and present as a bullet that has yet to penetrate his most vital organs. That isn't true, though, and he knows it. He's processing hurt the way he always has: going numb and letting it linger.

It will catch up with him later. He knows that. As long as he's not broken right now, he'll deal with it when it comes—and hopefully Jack won't have to see the ensuing fallout, which will be messy and explosive.

He focuses on the bright colors of the television, the pretty reporter in her crisp suit as she talks into a microphone for the camera's benefit. It takes a minute for her words to sink into his muddled brain.

"In the aftermath of the explosion that rocked Larkin's Bar on Grey Street yesterday evening, authorities say eight people have died. At least five more are missing, and police are asking for help locating the missing patrons whose names appear at the bottom of this screen. The cause of the explosion remains unknown. Anyone with any information is encouraged to contact Inspector Grant Hawkins at the River Falls Police Department—"

The television goes dark, and Jack tosses the remote onto the other side of the couch. George's gaze doesn't stray from the empty screen.

The burden is getting heavier. The numbness in his chest shifts like thawing ice, and he feels his throat grow tight. Eight people... and more missing, eight people, including Matt and Alex. A mystery explosion that only he knows the cause of. *Eight people are dead.*

Slowly, George sits up. "I did this," he says in a voice that rings hollow. "I made the tear worse. I summoned you again. It was me."

"Hey, no. George." Jack crouches in front of him, seizing his chin to force him to look at him. George doesn't want to meet those dark, intense eyes, but he has no choice. "Don't do that shit. Don't you dare."

"They're all dead because of me—"

"You don't know that."

"I do. Jack, it was after me. Matt distracted it, but it wanted to kill *me*." He closes his eyes, exhales out a whimper, and forces a manic grin. "I have never screwed up this badly in my life!"

When he starts to laugh, it's almost cathartic. He feels Jack recoil, confused by the unpredictability of human emotions. Or maybe it's just George's emotions—maybe he really is splintered, screwed up, broken beyond repair. Maybe he was that way before he started this whole demon mess to begin with.

Jack gives him the space until George's laughing has turned into ragged gasps, and he's hunched over with his head between his knees as he struggles not to cry. Losing it won't help anyone. They deserve more than that. Matt and Alex deserve better.

After he remembers how to breathe again, he goes still. He hears Jack in the kitchen, bustling around, but he doesn't say anything to him even when he emerges minutes later and presses a hot mug into his hand. George is grateful for both gestures. He takes a sip of the most bitter coffee he's ever tasted—if this is what Jack is used to, hell must be an awful place—and lets the liquid warm his insides before he sets it down.

He's almost too distracted to hear his phone ringing the first few times. Only when he notices it lit up against the coffee table does he realize the world hasn't stopped, just because he has. He has no intention of answering until he sees Josh's name on the screen. Then he forces himself to.

"Hello?" His voice is hoarse—God, he must sound awful.

To be fair, the speaker on the other end of the line doesn't sound much better. "Hey—George," Josh greets, sounding exhausted, and a little shaky. "Umm, how're you doing?"

George doesn't remember what happened to Josh last night. When police lights had begun flashing from down the street, his friend had gravitated towards them; Jack and George retreated away. The last he saw of Josh, he was still clutching Matt's ring and muttering to himself.

The question is ludicrous. "How are you doing"—as if either of them could really be okay right now. George huffs a strained half laugh and feels a little like he's going crazy. "I dunno, Josh. How're you doing?"

"I'm..." Josh hesitates, swallows the answer on the tip of his tongue, and inhales loud enough that George can hear it through the phone. "Well. Look, I've got a question. What was the name of that bookstore we went to, on your birthday? Do you remember?"

George's brow furrows. Whatever he expected, it wasn't that. "The bookstore? Hell, I don't remember—" He has to think for a minute. *"Hex's* or something? I wasn't paying attention. Why do you wanna know that?"

A moment of silence passes, a few seconds too long, before Josh says, "Thanks, George."

George has had it up to here by being jerked around by people who don't feel like telling him something. If Josh thinks he can get away with that too, he's got another thing coming. "Josh. Why do you want to know?"

He can hear Josh scrambling for something believable on the other end of the line. Josh has always been an awful liar—he's got a hell of a poker face when actually gambling, but when it comes to being dishonest with his friends he's a fish on dry land. George knows every one of Josh's tells even without being able to see him, so when he hears the drawn out, *"Well,"* before his explanation, he knows he's hearing a lie. "I'm just... writing the memories down. It's helping, I think. I want to... I can't stand to lose them. What we have left of them, I mean."

It's dishonesty, but the words strike a chord in George all the same. He isn't about to press. What's the point? He sighs into the phone, feeling something inside him wilt. "Yeah. I feel you. Stay out of trouble, okay?"

"You too, Soto." Josh doesn't sound relieved. He sounds... hollow. "Call me if you need me."

The line disconnects, and George is left staring down at his darkened phone in confusion. He wills it to ring again; for the face to light up with the dumb selfie Matt set as his contact photo the last time he stole George's phone, or for the candid shot that Alex can't stand to flash on the screen. If he could just hear their voices, be reassured that this is all some awful dream....

His fingers itch. He's two seconds away from dialing one of the numbers he knows won't answer, just to hear it ring. Just for the chance, the idiotic, impossible hope that's eating away at him.

He passes the phone over to Jack, not looking up. "Take this before I do something stupid."

Jack takes his phone, and not a word is said about it.

THE HOURS WIND by—morning into afternoon, afternoon into night. As the sun begins to fall and the apartment is cast into shadow, it's Jack who combats the encroaching darkness. He darts around the apartment, flicking on lights wherever he finds one; he nearly trips over George's cat more than once in his haste to keep the room from growing too dark.

"Dora, knock it off," George mutters, sure that she's trying to get in Jack's way. "You're being a pain."

Jack flicks on one final light before settling down on the couch, content that they're sitting in the most brightly lit apartment in the whole city. He watches the cat duck into the closet and vanish from sight. "You named your cat Dora?"

"Yeah," George nods; and just because it's a joke he's told before, and one that comes easy to him, he says, "after Pandora. You know, like the box?"

"Seriously?"

"Oh yeah, she used to get into everything. It was wild. I found her in the shower, the fridge—once she even got in the oven. No one knows how she did it, but then she'd get stuck places and be pissed at me. Eventually I named her that in case she took the hint. Dora just kinda worked."

Jack starts laughing. It's real, honest laughter, open and uninhibited, coming from deep within Jack's chest. He doubles over his own lap with it. What George said wasn't even that funny, but Jack is so relieved to hear him making jokes that he'll take anything he can get.

Jack has a beautiful laugh. Hearing it makes something twist in George's chest.

A part of him resents Jack for sticking with him all day. It wasn't enough that Jack had to save his ass in the bar; ever since, he hasn't left George's side. He's babied him, looked after him, and George knows he has no right to insist that he doesn't need it. Jack has been a lifesaver, literally, and it makes him angry because Jack still lied to him. Jack is still contracted to him, and he hasn't told George the truth yet.

George only wants to hear the truth. Even a little bit, a part of it—as long as it comes from Jack's lips.

He waits for the demon's laughter to die off. "Jack," he says, "I want you to tell me what was in that bar."

Jack goes still.

He wants to feel bad for killing whatever mood there was so abruptly, but he needs to know. They need to talk about this, and if they don't, they never will. "I need to know," he continues, "because I'm pretty sure I caused it."

Jack looks at him, eyes hooded. He looks tired all of a sudden, and George isn't surprised. He's been hiding his own exhaustion all day for his benefit. "It wasn't your fault, George," he mutters. "That thing wasn't a real demon. It didn't have a will of its own."

"What was it, then?"

"High-level demons—stronger than me—can make things out of demonic energy. Monsters. You know there are some demons who don't like humans, right?" George nods. He knows that pretty damn well at this point. "Well, the thing in the bar was something they made and sent here. It's what we call a chaos entity—something made to destroy whatever it can. That's all it does."

"So it blew up the bar—and Matt and Alex—" George feels sick. He presses a hand over his mouth, closing his eyes and trying not to think of pools of blood drenching the ground. He hears Jack hum.

"It wasn't you, George. You didn't cause it."

"It could have come through the tear. How else could it have gotten through?"

"Anyone can make a tear. You think you're the only one, George? The demon-human barrier isn't that strong. It's fragile. Down in hell, there are whole sectors—the ones that hate humans—who'd rather rip it down and save the trouble of maintaining it."

"Damn," George says, and gives a humorless chuckle. "These guys sound like real delights."

"We call them the Greys," Jack replies, disdain heavy in his tone. "Of the nine sectors of hell, the Greys control three of them. They stand for a lot of things, but hating humans is the biggest part."

"Sure lucky I didn't summon one of them."

"No. You summoned me." In a bold move, Jack lays a hand on George's shoulder. George can't help the way he tenses up. "I'm glad, George. I'm happy you summoned me."

For Jack, that's as good as saying "I love you."

George feels sick all over again. He closes his eyes, inhales a shaky breath, and forces out the words he knows he needs to say. "Jack, I want you to tell me the price of a contract."

Jack's hand pulls back all at once, as if George stung him. The mood hasn't been killed—George has *destroyed* it, seizing it around the neck and slamming it against the wall for it to shatter like a glass doll. When Jack meets his eyes again there is no way to mistake the pain there, the desperation to talk about anything but this. George won't give in.

"You know," Jack says quietly. "You know, George."

"Yeah," George says, and swallows hard, because he's figured it out by now and desperately wishes it weren't true. "But I've gotta hear you say it."

"I can't."

"It's your deal, so yeah," he bites out, "you can."

"For what—just to hurt you? Is that really what you want me to do?"

"You already hurt me! I just want you to fess up to it!"

"I didn't do a damn thing to you, and you know it! I could have hurt you, but I never did!"

"Why not?"

Jack's eyes are wide with anger, and maybe his words get ahead of his brain. "I don't ever want to hurt you!"

"Why not?" George demands again, throat feeling tight.

Jack tosses his hands up. "What do you mean, why not? Why do you think? You're—you're fucking *you!*"

"What does that mean?"

"It means you're stupid, and bratty, and annoying, and shameless, and you think you're way funnier than you actually are, and you're reckless but determined as all hell, and you laugh too much, and—and—" His voice twists, in some mangled imitation of laughter and pain all at once. He doubles forward, head between his knees, and sways like he's seasick. George starts to reach out to him but thinks better of it. "Jesus, you know, I don't know! You think I understand this? I'm a demon. I'm not supposed to care about anybody, humans least of all. I haven't got anyone to care about! No family—nothing. I'm a desk jockey, that's what I am, and I hate it. That's not what I was born for. I need... something to fight for. Then you came along, and you were different. You... made everything different."

His voice sounds agonized. It is as if he's choking on his own words but doesn't know how to stop. "All I know is I can't stand the thought of hurting you, or seeing you get hurt. Of losing you. When I pulled you out of that bar and thought you were dead, I swore—"

Jack cuts himself off; he's come to a dead end, nowhere to go and no more words to fall back on. He presses a hand over his face and remains still.

George swallows hard. It's so much to take in all at once, and his brain, overburdened and strung out as it is, struggles to handle it.

Every last lie Jack has told—from the omission of the contract's details to the seriousness of George's meddling—has been for one reason. George. Jack, for all his bitching, couldn't bear the thought of losing George. Even if George cannot forgive him for his lies, there is something noble in that.

Something heartwarming. Something that almost makes him understand, if not forgive him.

If Jack hadn't lied, George would never have broken the barrier. Matt and Alex would still be alive. There would be no demons, no exorcisms... no Jack.

God, maybe George is selfish, but even after all that's happened, he can't stomach the idea of his life without Jack in it.

He can't forgive him. All he can do is try to understand, and he thinks he almost can.

"So, all the secrecy... it was all because you care about me. Huh?"

The laugh Jack gives is brittle, crackling like dead leaves. "Yeah, I think I do."

Long fingers drag through George's messy bangs, brushing them back out of his face. He exhales a massive breath. "Wow."

"Wow," echoes Jack.

And—because he has to know, has to hear it out loud at least once—George says, "So when our first contract was up, and you showed up here to collect what was yours...."

"I found out how stupid you really were," Jack finishes. "And I just couldn't. I couldn't take a part of you."

"But you didn't tell me."

"I couldn't do that, George. I guess I... hoped you'd call me back. Dammit, I don't know." Jack's fist twitches; he looks like he wants to hit something.

He can't blame Jack for this, not really. This isn't a surprise; nor, at this point, is the fact that the price of a contract is something so heavy. Demons have no use for human money, for material goods. They don't need things like that; they don't want them. What did George think he was agreeing to?

"I thought I could keep anything bad from happening," Jack's says, and his voice is small. It's wrong to hear such a defeated tone from Jack's lips—so wrong, wrong, *wrong*, that George wants to burst out laughing all over again.

It's preposterous. This situation is completely crazy. No way is any of this actually happening. No way are his friends dead; no way has George messed with something he can't control; no way has he fallen in love with the demon who has a claim on his goddamn soul.

This is all too much. He doesn't know what's happening, but he feels like he's burning up inside. It's agony. It's fantastic. It's awful. It's amazing.

He feels everything all at once, and still he can only think of one thing to do.

Swooping in before Jack can react, George seizes his face in both hands and pulls him into a passionate kiss.

For one moment, Jack doesn't react. George is the one working against his lips, pushing, attacking him from every side he can. Of all the things Jack could have expected, this was probably never in the equation. Hell, George doesn't know what he's doing himself—all he knows is that he feels for Jack, such a whirlpool of emotions he hardly knows how to sort it out. Maybe this will make things clearer. Maybe Jack's mouth on his will hold all the answers that his words can't provide.

(Of course, there's also the fact that from the moment they first met, he's *really* wanted to kiss Jack.)

When Jack pulls away, the need inside George is so great that it aches. He's almost disappointed, until he sees the way Jack's dark eyes burn beneath hooded lids. "George," he mutters. The self-control it's taking him to keep himself back from George causes slight tremors to wrack his body. "What are you doing?"

George smiles against his mouth, feeling delirious. He doesn't know; at the same time, he's never been more sure of anything. "You want to take me?" he breathes. "Do it."

"I don't—"

When lips find his again, any last protests die in Jack's throat, and George swallows them down.

IN THE AFTERMATH, they curl together on the couch, lost in a world that holds the two of them alone. George lies pressed against a strong, solid chest. Jack has both muscular arms twined around George's shoulders, and every so often brushes feather-light kisses along the side of his neck.

On the other side of the living room, sitting propped up against the wall, is the giant plush monkey that Jack stole from the carnival. George had no clue what to do with it after getting it; he'd set it up next to the television, and never bothered to put it anywhere else. Its black glossy eyes stare at them, watchful but nonintrusive.

"Jack," George says, "I have to ask you something."

Jack hums. "What is it?"

"Why—" He starts, cuts himself off, and has to swallow back a grin. "Why did you get me a giant monkey?"

Without his glasses on, George can't make out the specifics of Jack's face; but he is certain he can see his blurry features twist, a flush spreading across his face. "I thought you'd like it." Jack sounds supremely embarrassed.

George rests his chin on Jack's collar, grinning broadly. "Let me guess. It reminded you of me."

"You're both small and annoying as hell, so yeah."

"Jack, that thing is as big as me. It's bigger than me. What's it done to annoy you anyway?"

"I don't like monkeys."

"But you like me?"

Jack's eyes fix on him for a long moment. Their intensity steals the breath from George's lungs. "Yeah," he says. "I do."

George is just starting to lean up, ready to steal another kiss, when their peace is shattered without warning. The phone rings, it's shrill chime splitting through the hush of the apartment.

"Oh, what the hell now?" George groans, disentangling himself from Jack. The demon still has an arm around his waist and seems very hesitant to let go. It takes no small amount of squirming to dislodge himself from Jack's iron grip, but the smirk on Jack's face makes it worth it.

George fumbles for his phone before raising it to his ear, not bothering to check the caller. "Whoever this is, you've got incredible timing. You deserve a damn award."

He is greeted with the sound of harsh breathing over the other end of the line. For a moment, that's all he hears; his brow furrows as he pushes himself up, trying to discern a voice amidst the mess of static and panting breaths.

When someone finally does speak, it's in a hushed, rushed whisper, thick with panic. "George! I messed up—oh shit, I messed up so bad, I didn't mean to, I didn't—oh, hell—"

George bolts upright, all postcoital bliss melting away in place of icy fear. He's only heard his friend sound so freaked out once before, and it was last night. "Josh! Slow down, what's going on?"

"I screwed up!" Josh exclaims, sounding like he's in tears. "I don't know what's happening!"

George stumbles away from the couch, tripping over his own feet in his haste to find his discarded clothes. His friend needs his help, and he's naked—Josh's timing really *is* perfect. "Where are you right now? I'll come get you."

"In the graveyard on West Street—" There is another shriek of static, then a shout that can only come from Josh. When he speaks into the phone again, his voice is distorted. "Something's chasing me! George, it's coming the hell after me!"

"What is? Josh!"

"What'd he do?" Jack demands, on his feet as well and leaning closer to the phone. George waves his hand helplessly, scrambling to zip his jeans one-handed. Jack passes him his coat without being asked, and George trips over his sneakers.

Josh doesn't stop rambling, but in the time it takes George to get dressed even seems to grow more frantic. Instead of words, the most that comes over the other line is his ragged breathing, with a few interspersed exclamations of panic.

"Josh!" George persists, racing for his apartment door. "Tell me what's going on, buddy!"

"I tried—" A strangled whimper escapes Josh's throat as his voice rises in pitch. "Matt—oh God, *Matt*—"

Then there is a sound on the other end of the line—an awful, definite sound, a cross between a siren wail and a screech of static. There is a gasp. The line goes dead.

"What about Matt?" George is still yelling into the phone. "Josh! Hey, hello? Answer me, dammit!"

No answer is forthcoming. The screen is dark, and George can do nothing but stare down at it in dismay. He is utterly helpless.

He feels something in him snap, and his phone is clattering down the hallway before he even knows he's thrown it. He kicks at the wall, face screwed up to hold back desperate tears. "Shit! Shit, shit!"

Jack's the one to grab him, pulling him back before he can shatter his foot. He must have been able to hear the conversation; his face is grim, and the black clothes he now wears are immaculately fresh-conjured. Jack holds George steady, arms around his shoulders as he brushes hair from his face. He is muttering soothing things, but George can't hear them.

"I can't," he gasps out, gripping Jack's arms tightly. "I can't lose him too. I can't, Jesus, Jack, I can't—"

"I'll take you," Jack says quickly, and George's mouth shuts with a click. Jack waits for some sort of agreement; when none is forthcoming, he prompts George with a nod. "Okay?"

George nods, feeling so strung out that he hardly knows what he's agreeing to. All he knows is that he needs to get to Josh. "Y-yeah. Okay."

The next thing he knows, Jack's grip tightens and the world around them both dissolves like watercolors blurring in a rainstorm. Everything seems to melt away all at once, fading to an all-consuming canvas of gray; there is no color, no wind, no sense of moving or falling. One second they are standing in George's apartment hallway, and the next they are in the middle of the cemetery at the end of West Street, and Jack is looking intently into George's face.

"You all right?"

George takes a moment to affirm that that really just happened before he's able to nod. He's okay—he's in one piece, at least—but he is also far from his own main concern. Immediately he finds himself reeling, gaze swiveling around the cemetery as he searches for any sign of his friend.

Josh isn't there. Amongst the rows of headstones, shrouded by the shadows of night, there is no sign of George's friend. The cemetery is deserted; the only signs of life are the sound of his and Jack's own heavy breathing and an owl hooting from the canopy of trees overhead.

George swallows anxiously and scans the vicinity once more. "He said he was here."

"I know. I heard him." Jack's voice sounds tense.

George doesn't know what he's doing—indeed, a part of him protests leaving Jack's side at all—but he finds himself wandering over to the great stone mausoleum resting at the center of the cemetery. He can't be sure what draws his attention there. Maybe it's instinct, or maybe he's smart enough by now to know to gravitate towards the creepiest place in the area. As he approaches the steps, however, and catches a glint of silver on the ground, he no longer hesitates.

There are a few things waiting to be found on the stone steps of the mausoleum. George frowns at the mess that litters the ground. There are some discarded cigarette butts, an empty bottle of what looks like whiskey, and a crumpled paper. Whoever was here before was either enjoying himself or having a really weird night; George has a brief hope that it wasn't Josh, but he realizes the whiskey is the same brand Josh always drinks when he wants to not remember tomorrow.

That's when his eyes catch on something that sends a real jolt of fear through him—a chalk circle on the top step. His stomach flips, and he nearly trips his way up to where he can see an array of sigils sketched out with a frantic hand. They're shaky but legible. Most alarming, however, is the small puddle of crimson blood that mars the pale stone in the center of the circle.

He mutters a curse to himself as he stoops to pick up the crumpled paper. It crinkles as he unravels it, the sound echoing in the air around him. A sharp inhale catches in his throat as he reads the title of the page, in spindly handwriting.

Methods of Resurrecting the Dead.

The bold headline is followed by what seems like a list of various forms of death magic, and a drawing of what looks a lot like the circle in front of them.

George feels his heart drop to the pit of his stomach. "This looks like the page I took to summon you," he says aloud, staring down at the crumpled paper. His eyes slowly widen in realization as his mind races, flashing back to Josh's questions from earlier. There's only one place this paper could have come from. If Josh really went back to the shop, and he *really* stole a spell to bring back the dead—

"And Matt's ring." George feels dizzy as he lifts the battered silver piece from the stone steps. By now, the ring is all but falling apart in his hands, but it is unmistakable. It is the one Matt wore every day with devoted pride, and the one he died with—lying here, at the front of a mausoleum, next to a spell about raising the dead.

He thinks of Josh, devastated after Matt and Alex's deaths. Josh, who'd been joined at the hip with Matt since college. Josh, who was always the one to text, to call, so determined to keep their friend group together....

Josh, devastated. Josh, desperate.

Slowly, he turns his head to look up at Jack. "What the hell happened here?"

"I had to do it."

The unexpected voice takes them both by surprise. George jumps, whirling around; Jack's arm shoots out to hold him back. Their eyes widen as they fall upon the figure standing in a row of tombstones only a few feet away.

George swallows hard. It feels like all the moisture has been sucked from his throat. "J-Josh?"

Josh is a wreck. His head is down, obscuring his face from sight. His hair hangs in his eyes, scraggly and unruly. It is matted with something that looks like dirt; the same substance smears his bare arms and face. There is a long cut on the lower part of his arm, as if he took a knife and dragged it across his skin. It leaks a steady trickle of blood to the ground at his feet, but Josh doesn't seem to notice. His shoulders are heaving; his breath comes out in strangled wheezes.

"I had to," Josh says again. He sounds more desperate this time, more like the Josh that sobbed to George on the phone, not this twisted apparition. "He couldn't be dead. He was my best friend. I thought I... could do it."

Jack is on edge, every muscle tense, nerves tuned to the surroundings. He lays a hand on George's arm, just firm enough to draw his attention. George lays a hand on top of Jack's own and squeezes.

"You wanted to bring him back," he says slowly. Josh doesn't react. "I get that. It's okay, buddy. But this isn't right. We've got to go home now."

"It's too late for that," Josh says, his voice going small and flat. "Too late. Too late."

"What do you mean?" Jack's hand tightens on his arm. "What do you mean, Josh?"

Josh twitches once, like he's taking a deep breath. "It's too late," he says again, voice ringing like a bell in the silent graveyard. "He's here."

Josh lifts his head, revealing a nightmare. His eyes are pitch black, sunken into a waxy, sallow face. Black veins pulse at his temples and neck. When he opens his mouth, it is a black hole lined with glistening bullets, utterly inhuman. The noise that comes out is not a sob; it is a roar.

George lets out a yell at the same time Jack jerks him backwards. They wind up behind the mausoleum, out of view of Josh—or the thing wearing Josh's face. It is not his friend, no matter how it might look. This is something George knows for certain. Josh is not possessed, but that thing behind them was more of a demonic echo than the real product. Josh is...

Josh isn't here. Josh is gone, the same way Matt is, and Alex. Whatever that thing behind them is has been left in Josh's place.

Except when George pokes his head out from behind the mausoleum, he sees that the Thing That Is Not Josh has vanished too. There is a puddle of black blood where it used to be. Other than that, nothing remains. He holds his breath as he turns back to Jack, eyes wide.

"I don't like this," Jack says. "We've got to get out of here."

"But Josh—"

"That *wasn't Josh*." Jack is emphasizing what George already knows, but the very real fear in his voice takes him aback. "George, there's something here. I can feel it. I don't know what it is, but it's not something good. It feels like—"

A small tremor shakes the ground. Jack cuts himself off, eyes widening.

George turns to look at him in confusion, but before he can open his mouth, Jack has a hand on his back and is shoving him forward. "Go!" he exclaims. "Run, move it!"

"What the hell is going on?" Another tremor rocks the cemetery, and George nearly loses his balance. Earthquakes in Rhode Island? That just doesn't *happen.* There's no way this could be natural, unless—

Unless it isn't.

He looks back at Jack to find absolute panic written across his face. That's all George is able to register before a much larger shockwave knocks him off his feet.

He is sent to the ground in a tumble of flailing limbs, coming close to knocking his head against a gravestone. Instead, he lands hard on his shoulder. A sharp ache shoots through his side, but this is minor compared to the way the entire earth rumbles beneath him like it's trying to shake every living thing off.

Someone yells his name, and then Jack is on the ground at his side. He has a hand on George's back, but any other words he says are drowned out by thunder crashing in the sky. George can only nod to show that he's all right. When Jack reaches for him, he grips him back. Jack is reassuringly solid in contrast to the rattling earth; George wishes he could bury his face in Jack's chest and return to that peaceful little world of only the two of them, for just one more minute.

There's no time for that. Their peace is gone. Now the entire earth is splitting in two, and George is seized with the sudden certainty that out of all the ways he has come close to dying in the past few days, this will be it. There is something so awful in this moment, something that screams to him that it is the end of the world. He is filled with a dread so overwhelming, so suffocating, that he has to press his face into Jack's shoulder just to breathe.

Jack's grip grounds him. He doesn't know if the demon is talking anymore, but he is still steady, so very solid. For as long as the shaking holds out, Jack holds him and refuses to let go. For a few agonizing seconds, it seems like it will never end.

Then there is the sudden feeling of the air being sucked forward—stolen from George's mouth, his lungs, as if he never held claim on it in the first place. He sucks in a breathless gasp, and Jack holds him tighter. Even behind his closed eyelids, George can see a flash of bright light, and hear a horrible roar echoing in his ears.

The pressure rises and rises, until George is sure his eardrums will burst and his chest will explode. He can hear Jack grunting against him, withstanding the force. George cannot even bring himself to lift his head.

Then, just as suddenly, the chaos stops. The world goes quiet again. Everything is still; everything is silent. He can breathe.

When George lifts his head from Jack's chest, he expects to find chaos all around them. Instead of being confronted with torn up headstones and fallen trees, however, he is met with a serene sight. The ground is level and unharmed; the trees, bearing all their branches, still stand tall. It is like the tremor never happened in the first place.

Or, at least, it *would* be—if the great stone mausoleum that stood tall just minutes ago was not now splintered through the middle, a giant crack causing each half of the stone to slump to the side.

George's eyes widen as he takes in the broken mausoleum. Compared to the destruction he was expecting, this is nothing—yet dread boils in the pit of his stomach at the mere sight, and a chill runs up his spine.

"What the hell was that?" he manages to gasp out.

Jack looks grim. There is a darkness to his face that George has never seen, solemnity that makes him look centuries older. His face is lined. His eyes are shadowed. He stares at the fractured mausoleum as if he cannot look away.

"Pretty sure," he says, "that was the start of the apocalypse."

OF ALL THE things George Soto did not sign up for, the apocalypse is at the very top of the list.

"What the hell was that?" he's still saying, even after Jack has magicked them both back to George's apartment and bolted the doors behind them. "What *was* that? Jack, where's Josh, what the holy hell was *that?*"

"Shut up." Jack is pacing the length of the summoning circle, tense enough to wear tracks into the wood. He has his hands balled at his sides; his shoulders are tense, face set in an unreadable mask. George falls back at the dismissal, but it's obvious Jack has bigger things on his mind.

"Jack, I mean it," he says after another few minutes of pacing make it clear the demon isn't about to tell him anything. "Tell me what just happened."

Finally, Jack rounds on him. He doesn't look angry; instead, there is a focus on his face that startles George. "I told you how fragile the barrier is. You're worried about a tiny tear? What you just saw was someone dragging a knife through it and slashing it up."

"Oh." George drags the word out for a solid few seconds. "That's... bad."

"Yeah, that's bad." Ferocity bleeds through Jack's tone. "I don't even know how many demons just got out of there, but I know they were Greys. If they came through to the human world like that, it means there's a war on our hands. Hell is about to have a war, and humans will be caught in the middle."

George's head is reeling. He lowers himself to the couch slowly, unsure of what to do. He is so far out of his depth here that it almost hurts. He understands more than he ever wanted to about possessions, demons, and magic—but the idea that there's an entire world he can't comprehend, and a war that could come to affect their world, is almost too much to process.

"What—what'll happen now?"

"Our side's gonna work to seal the barrier again, but like fuck will the Greys let that happen without a fight. It's gonna be chaos down here, and as long as that thing stays open the worse it'll get up here."

George runs a hand through his hair as Jack lashes out, kicking at the wall. His toe bounces off and he curses, though George knows it's not because of the pain.

"You've gotta go," says George. "You've gotta help your side."

"I can't, George."

"Why the hell not?"

"Because—" Jack cuts himself off, face distorting in an expression so pained that George wonders if he bit his tongue. When he is finally able to spit out the words, they are tight and forced. "I'm contracted to you. You're my—my *problem* until the contract ends, and I'm not gonna do that. As long as I'm tied to you, I can't go down and fight."

George snorts at the absurdity of Jack's words. "What are you gonna do here, huh?"

"I'll protect you," Jack says, sounding like he's trying very hard to be assured. "If anything tries to hurt you— you've still got the tear, so if anything tries to get through—"

There is a rock in George's stomach, growing heavier with each word Jack utters. He's learned to recognize when Jack's stubbornness is at its peak; this, he realizes, is something far more grievous. Not only is the contract preventing Jack from taking his place where he really belongs—at the frontlines, defending his world along with his comrades—but Jack can't stand the idea of leaving George. Not that George can blame him. After everything, he doesn't want to be alone either.

That's what will happen if Jack leaves. He'll be all alone.

His closest friends are dead or missing. His family is hundreds of miles away. If Jack leaves too....

George won't have anyone.

He can't stand the idea of losing Jack, but he needs to let him go. He has to let him fight, and in order to do that....

The contract needs to be broken.

"Jack, how do I close the tear?" he demands. If Jack notices the fresh sense of urgency in his voice, he doesn't react to it. His pacing continues, wearing tracks in George's floor—literally. His feet are beginning to smoke with the pent-up tension Jack has no outlet to release. He waves his hand in front of him, so deep in thought he hardly seems to realize the question.

"If you wanna do that, you need to destroy the circle, and I have to take my end of the contract. That's the only way. But who knows how big the tear is, especially compared to the goddamn portal to hell that just opened up—"

He cuts himself off. That's when the words hit him, and he finally goes still. Jack's jaw grinds; his fists flex, once, twice, three times at his side. He inhales a breath and then exhales it in a harsh rush of air. Every inch of him is dripping with frustration. He is like a coiled wire, ready to snap at any time. Jack is being torn apart by his need to be with his people—only restricted by the contract that binds him.

You have to let him go, George reminds himself again, and swallows down the bitterness coating his tongue.

"There's a war, Jack," he says, voice soft and flat. "We both know it's where you belong."

Jack says nothing. His silence stings, burning George like a hot iron. Still, he forces himself to his feet and tries not to let his hesitation slow him as he steps into the circle and towards Jack. "Well, I guess there's only one thing we can do."

Surprise is clear on Jack's face as George steps right up to him, leaving barely a few inches of space between their chests. George has to crane his neck to regard Jack's face, but he could almost smile at how baffled the demon looks. Jack is awkward when it comes to physical affection and has a habit of being clueless when least expected; just a few of the many things George has come to love about him.

"George..." George's actions have left Jack breathless. Hands seize him by the shoulders, preventing him from getting any closer. "George, what are you doing?"

"You need to be somewhere else, Jack," George says, and smiles although it agonizes him to do so. "You have to go."

"I can't, not as long as I'm still tied to you—"

"We've just gotta fix that, then," George says, and loops his arms around Jack's neck. The demon is too stunned to pull away.

"What're you—" he starts, but George doesn't let him finish. He stares Jack dead in the face, fighting not to lose himself in the dark pools of his eyes, and forces the command out before he can think better of it.

"Jack. Take my soul."

The direct order clicks into place, the same way George knew it would. He sees Jack's eyes widen, feels the instinctual obedience in the way Jack's hands seize the backs of his shoulders and grip hard. It hurts; George holds his breath, preparing for whatever is to come, but Jack snaps out of it before he can act.

"No—" Jack looks horrified, furious, as he returns to himself. He tries to pull back, but George's determined grip won't let him. "The fuck, *no,* I won't fuckin' *do that—*"

"Take my soul, Jack. Then destroy the circle, then go."

The next order doesn't have the same effect. Jack was expecting it, and keeps himself from giving in. He still has a grip on the back of George's shoulders, though, possessive fingers bruising the skin even further. George doubts he could pull away if he tried. *"Stop,"* the demon spits, craning his head to keep from looking George in the face. Pain distorts his voice into something more demonic than human. It doesn't scare George anymore; now, he only accepts this part of Jack, as he's accepted what has to come next.

"You need to do this," George presses, motor-mouth never letting him down—even when he's on the brink of death. "We both know why this has to happen. There's no way around it, you tried, and Jesus, Jack, I don't wanna lose you either, but if this is how it has to end...."

Jack's face contorts, like he's fighting the urge to cry. It feels like a knife in George's chest. "I *can't...*"

"I know."

And before he can start crying, before he can choke on his own words and fall apart against Jack's chest, George presses his mouth to Jack's in a fervent kiss. He clutches the demon like he never wants to let him go, and he *doesn't*. Jack feels the same, because he clings to George even as the other man pulls away just enough to allow breaths to pass between their parted mouths.

There's a lot he wishes he could say. He's never had a problem expressing himself with his mouth; words are so important to him, can say so much. He wants to tell Jack everything, every little thought and feeling he's had since the moment he saw him. He wants to say so much: *I understand. It's okay. I love you.* He wants to repeat every word he's ever said, relive every second, but in this moment all he has is Jack's agonized gaze. For the first time in his life, the words George so desperately wants to command will not come.

Instead, George offers a small smile. "See ya around, Jack."

Jack squeezes his eyes shut, exhaling a quavering sigh against his mouth. "George…"

George closes his eyes too and doesn't take a breath before he leans forward once more. *"Do it,"* he orders against Jack's lips and then falls into a last feverish kiss.

Falling… *falling.* That's what it feels like. He feels the second Jack breaks, the moment he gives himself up to his last act of obedience. George feels the pain in his chest as something inside of him is tugged, short and sharp. Then there is a moment of world-shattering dizziness. Darkness swallows him up. And then…

George is falling.

The last thing he feels is himself, slumping bonelessly into Jack's arms, but that last touch fades away like the caress of a summer breeze. George falls into nothing and feels no more.

Epilogue

GEORGE—GEORGE'S BODY, the shell that used to be George, the thing that once held so much life when George Soto still existed—makes no sound as Jack lowers it to the ground.

His arms feel empty now that they are devoid of the persistent weight pressing into them. The skin upon which George breathed is still warm. His lips are on fire from that final kiss. He can feel bile creeping up his throat; he forces it back down, along with the ragged breath that threatens to burst out. He clenches his fists to hide their tremors, straightens his spine, and sets his shoulders.

The circle is destroyed quickly; he wipes away the chalk lines, sweeps the candles to the sides, and even scuffs his foot over the bloodstains on the floor. They will not come out, no matter how hard he tries to scrub. A small part of George will remain in this apartment forever.

He lays what once was George out flat, arms at his sides. If he didn't know better, he could tell himself he's only sleeping; but Jack has seen George sleep, a hot mess of tangled limbs and airy snores. He has not passed out in the middle of the floor after a long day at work, succumbing to exhaustion with a low murmur of, *"M not even that tired, just gotta lie down for a minute...."* He will not open his eyes and smile that broad, fearless smile when he finds Jack standing over him.

He is gone.

George is not the first human Jack has seen die. He is not the first he has killed. He will not be the last. Jack allows his fingers to linger over George's cool brow for just a second before he forces himself to pull away and rises from his crouch at the dead man's side. He takes a moment to feel the power flowing through his veins, to allow the magic that drives his body to stir and awaken.

He has been sleeping for far too long.

There is a war to fight, and at his heart, Jack has never been a "demonic pencil-pusher"—he is a soldier. He knows exactly where he needs to be now, and exactly what he must do.

He fades into the shadows as if he were never here at all, and leaves what is no longer George Soto behind.

THE FIRST THING he feels is electricity shooting through his veins.

His entire body seizes, and only when he slams back onto the ground is he stunned into awareness. Wide eyes stare up at a dark sky, cast over with storm clouds yet still illuminated by the bright light of the moon. Streetlights shine from somewhere not far away, but the street he finds himself in the middle of is dark.

He tries to sit up but finds he cannot. His entire body feels like lead. His muscles ache, and despite the small shocks of adrenaline he can feel coursing through his limbs he finds he does not have enough energy to move.

Rain pounds upon the concrete, lashing his bare skin. He is hot and cold all at once; he feels like he's burning up, even though he is conscious of the fact that he is lying naked in the middle of the street.

What happened? How did he get here? He presses his mind for memories, but a lance of white-hot pain shoots through his head and drowns everything else out. He tries to scream, but all that comes out is a garbled moan from a parched, brittle throat.

He has no clue what's happening, or why, but Beck Murray knows one thing for certain: *he shouldn't be here.*

About the Author

Emilie Lucadamo has too many stories, and not enough words to tell them. At eighteen years old, she has been writing for most of her life, and telling stories even longer. Her dream is to one day become a critically acclaimed author. When not writing, she's probably reading, or spending quality time with her dog.

Twitter: @EmilieLucadamo

Tumblr: www.emiliesbooks.tumblr.com

Coming Soon from Emilie Lucadamo

The Cost of Living

Excerpt

At first he thinks it's a news article—it is dated a few days after January first, New Year's Day. Some instinct tells him this is recent. When he focuses on the picture at the top of the article, Beck feels his heart stop.

It's his face—his bright eyes, his warm smile beaming beneath a headline that reads *"In Loving Memory of Thomas Becker Murray (1995 - 2017)"*.

For a long moment Beck cannot move. He stares at the article, wide-eyed and breathless. It's your standard obituary: when he died, who he leaves behind, a few spare facts about him, and where services will be held. His whole life and death boiled down to barely a paragraph. His own grin mocks him from the top of the page.

"That... was two months ago," he breathes, pointing at the picture. It was taken at his brother's last birthday party, in October. It had been a group shot—he and his friends, all posed in front of the camera.

Adam's brows are furrowed, expression closed off and unreadable. "Beck, this article was written in January. It's July now. You've been dead for seven months."

Beck's world drops out from under him.

Also Available from NineStar Press

Connect with NineStar Press

Website: NineStarPress.com

Facebook: NineStarPress

Facebook Reader Group: NineStarNiche

Twitter: @ninestarpress

Tumblr: NineStarPress

www.ingramcontent.com/pod-product-compliance
Lightning Source LLC
Chambersburg PA
CBHW050533190726
48284CB00003B/1051